YEARLING BOOKS

Since 1966, Yearling has been the

leading name in classic and award-winning

literature for young readers.

With a wide variety of titles,

Yearling paperbacks entertain, inspire,

and encourage a love of reading.

MERIDIAN MIDDLE SCHOOL

VISIT

WWW.RANDOMHOUSE.COM/KIDS

**TO FIND THE PERFECT BOOK, PLAY GAMES,
AND MEET FAVORITE AUTHORS!**

OTHER YEARLING BOOKS YOU WILL ENJOY

ON MY HONOR
Marion Dane Bauer

JOHNNY TREMAIN
Esther Forbes

HATTIE BIG SKY
Kirby Larson

MR. TUCKET
Gary Paulsen

WHERE THE RED FERN GROWS
Wilson Rawls

HOLES
Louis Sachar

THE SIGN OF THE BEAVER
Elizabeth George Speare

BELLE PRATER'S BOY
Ruth White

THE HERO
Ron Woods

HEART
OF A
SHEPHERD

ROSANNE PARRY

A YEARLING BOOK

Copyright © 2009 by Rosanne Parry

All rights reserved. Published in the United States by Yearling,
an imprint of Random House Children's Books, a division of Random House, Inc., New York.
Originally published in hardcover in the United States by Random House Children's Books,
a division of Random House, Inc., New York, in 2009.

Yearling and the jumping horse design are registered trademarks of Random House, Inc.

Visit us on the Web! www.randomhouse.com/kids

Educators and librarians, for a variety of teaching tools, visit us
at www.randomhouse.com/teachers

Library of Congress Cataloging-in-Publication Data
Parry, Rosanne.
Heart of a shepherd / Rosanne Parry.
p. cm.
Summary: Ignatius "Brother" Alderman, nearly twelve, promises to help his grandparents keep
the family's Oregon ranch the same while his brothers are away and his father is deployed to Iraq,
but as he comes to accept the inevitability of change, he also sees the man he is meant to be.
ISBN 978-0-375-84802-5 (trade) — ISBN 978-0-375-94802-2 (lib. bdg.) —
ISBN 978-0-375-84803-2 (pbk.) — ISBN 978-0-375-89250-9 (e-book)
[1. Ranch life—Oregon—Fiction. 2. Responsibility—Fiction.
3. Family life—Oregon—Fiction. 4. Christian life—Fiction. 5. Iraq War, 2003– —Fiction.
6. War—Fiction. 7. Oregon—Fiction.] I. Title.
PZ7.P248Hea 2009 [Fic]—dc22 2007048094

Printed in the United States of America

10 9 8 7 6 5 4 3

First Yearling Edition

For Bill, who came home

CONTENTS

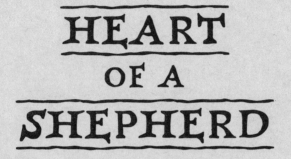

HEART
OF A
SHEPHERD

THE CHESS MEN

JULY

Grandpa frowns when he plays chess, like he does when he prays. He's got a floppy mustache that pulls that frown right down past his chin. He used to have freckles like me, but I guess they expanded on him because his whole face is pack-mule tan, with a fan of wrinkles at the corners. Years and years of moving cattle and mending fences gives a man a fearsome look, and I bet if I work at it, I can look just like my grandpa by the time I go to board at the high school. But the fences are mended for now and the cows are up in the mountains with my older brothers, so Grandpa and me are playing chess out on the back porch.

Grandpa's chessmen are world-famous around here. They came over the Oregon Trail with Grandpa's grandfather in the covered wagon, and before that they came straight from Paris, France. They were carved by hand from ebony for the dark side and ivory for the light. The pawns all have round helmets and longbows. Everyone else has a sword, even the bishops, and their faces are dead serious, which is what you want when there's a war on.

Grandpa is the chess champ of Malheur County, Oregon. We've been playing each other for years, so I've got him pretty well sized up. He always opens by moving the middle pawn up two spaces. But after that first move, he's as wily as a badger and twice as tough. I haven't beaten him yet, but when I do, it will be worth a town parade.

Now, to my mind, pawns are a shifty-looking bunch, plus they clutter up the board, so I try to clear most of them off right away, his and mine. I like my knights to have plenty of room to ride. My queen's knight rides a paint mustang. That horse has got a temper; she's lean and fast, and brave as a lion. My king's knight rides a Clydesdale; not so much speed, but plenty of power.

Rosita's my queen, of course. She's a fifth grader up at the school, and my best friend's sister. She can birth a lamb and kill a rattlesnake with a slingshot, which is what I look for in a queen. Plus, she's as pretty as a day in spring, and she laughs when I'm the one talking.

I bet Grandpa's working on putting me in a fork. That's his favorite move, but I see it coming a mile away, so I take a sip from a sweaty glass of lemonade and talk things over with the men. My king's bishop is all for killing Grandpa's queen before she can get us, because, after all, he is an excellent swordsman. The trouble is, Grandpa's queen would have to be Grandma, and I couldn't let anything bad happen to her, now could I? It's confession for sure, for killing your grandma.

My queen's bishop and I talk the other bishop out of it, which we do a lot. The queen's bishop is the more reflective type because his hands are carved together for praying.

Grandpa leans forward in his straight-backed chair, still frowning. Dad's orders sit on the card table beside the chessboard, in a tan army envelope. I made Dad show me, because I couldn't believe what he said. They're going to send him and the entire 87th Transportation Battalion all the way to Iraq. Reserve guys are only supposed to go places for two weeks—maybe three, if there's a hurricane in Texas. Fourteen months! It says Dad will be gone fourteen months, right in print. Like this is going to sound better to me than Dad is going to miss my birthday two years in a row.

Grandma's got him in the kitchen. I can hear the buzz of the clippers through the screen door. She takes about two minutes to cut my hair, but she's been at it with Dad for half an hour. I think she just wants an excuse to rub some extra blessings into his head. I hope she keeps him in there for an hour. He's going to need all the blessings he can get in Baghdad.

Grandpa pauses so long in the game, I get to wondering if he's even playing. He's been writing letters to our senator to oppose the war ever since it started. Half the Quaker congregations west of the Mississippi have signed them. Grandpa is not an out-loud worrier like Grandma. He just spends more time in the evening praying and writing in his journal.

"He doesn't really have to go, does he?"

Grandpa looks up from the board, straight at me.

"He took a vow when he put on that uniform. A promise is a binding thing, Brother, before the law and before God, too."

"God doesn't believe in war, does he? You don't."

"Protest is my calling. Your dad's is to take care of the men in his command. He can be faithful in that."

The sun is just starting to go orange, and the wind

settles down like it does this time of day. The whole ranch gets quiet, like it's waiting for the next move. Grandpa scoots his bishop up three spaces. He looks at me and smiles.

A fork! I knew it. My queen's in danger! Her knight is on the other end of the fork. What'll I do?

The queen's bishop starts right in on his rosary, and my two remaining pawns fit an arrow to the bow, but King Grandpa doesn't flinch.

My king's bishop is a string of bad advice, and my king's knight says, "It's a rough spot, laddie, but one or the other of them will have to go. You know it's true."

Both horses nod solemnly in agreement.

"But, Your Highness," says the queen's knight, "there's a way out, Your Majesty. I could ride up behind King Grandpa, and he wouldn't see me. Just let me take two turns. Come on."

I see what he's driving at, except it still wouldn't save my queen. Knights are brave enough in a battle, but they're not too bright, which you can tell by the way their eyebrows are all carved into one straight line.

"Think it over, Brother. Don't rush into anything," Grandpa says, which is what a man usually says when he'd like you to get on with it. But Grandpa's good at waiting, for a grown-up. He leans an elbow on the porch rail and stares out at the bluff where we've been finding cougar tracks all month long.

My queen just looks at me with those serious brown eyes and the long curly black hair. She likes me, I know she does. And what's better, she's trusting me to do the right thing. I stroke her hair with my finger just once, so she knows I like her too, and then I slide my king up one space, right between Rosita and her attacker.

"You can't move into check," Grandpa says.

"Yes, sir," I say, sitting tall on my barrel and slapping dust out of my jeans. "If you want me off this square, you're going to have to fight me."

"Well done, sir! Oh, bravely done!" shout my knights.

My king's bishop bows his head. "Your sacrifice will be remembered for all eternity."

The queen's bishop starts warming up the last rites.

The dead pawns at my feet send up a cheer, but I can hardly hear them because she smiled at me! A little wooden smile as tender as a snowflake on my eyelashes. I'm so proud I could bust. Grandpa looks from me to my queen, and back at me again. He smiles a little.

"Are you sure you want to play it this way, Brother?"

"Yup." Is he kidding? I never get to be the hero.

"Checkmate."

I did it! The game's over, and my queen is still standing!

Grandpa just shakes his head, but I can't stop smiling. Dad wanders over, brushing haircut stubble off his shirt. He gives my shoulder a squeeze.

"Fourteen months is a long time. We should talk," Dad says.

Grandpa gets up, straps on his tool belt, and heads up to the barn to fix the lamb pen. I can hear Grandma moving the pots and pans around in the kitchen and whistling some old Irish tune. Dad looks out at his land. Red Rock Creek comes down from the reservoir, a mile to the north, and flat green pasture stretches across the canyon floor to the dry hills on either side. There's a stand of willows by the water, and one giant cottonwood shades the south end of the barn and holds up my tire swing.

"Did you beat your grandpa at chess yet?" Dad says.

"Not exactly."

"Never mind, Brother. I think I was about fifteen before I won my first game."

Everybody calls me Brother because I've got four big brothers. My real name is Ignatius. Guess they ran out of all the good saints by the time they got to me. Lots of things ran out by the time they got to me. My brother Frank says it could be worse—they could have picked Augustine or Cyril—but honest, I wouldn't have minded being Gus, or even Cy. But Ignatius pretty much shortens to "Ig" or "Natius." That's not even a good name for a cow. Heck, I wouldn't name a pig either one.

"So what do you think?" Dad says, nodding in the direction of the envelope with his orders.

"I can't believe it. You've been in the reserves forever, and they've never asked you to do anything like this. Jeez, Grandma was in the reserves for thirty years, and they never sent her to a war."

People are going to be talking about this all over the county. There's a list of a hundred names in Dad's command. How's he going to tell all those families their dads are going to leave? Every volunteer fireman in a hundred miles is on that list. Our postmaster; the school janitor; the basketball coach; Arnie, who owns the only gas station in town; and every member of the

8

school board is on that list. A month from now, they'll all be on a plane.

I line the chessmen up in their box and sit on the porch rail next to Dad. I rub his bristle-short hair. He used to have red hair like mine, but what's left after Grandma's clippers is mostly gray fuzz. Dad looks up at the hills. He's standing more like a soldier already.

"What if your men don't want to go?"

"It's our mission, and we'll see it done."

Dad says it flat and cold, like a person isn't even allowed to think about not going. The chickens begin their nightly parade up from the banks of the creek behind the house to the chicken shed next to the barn out front.

"Paco and Rosita's mom and dad are on that list. It's not fair they both have to go. Rosita's too little to have her mom gone."

Truth is, every other kid in Dad's battalion has a mom at home, everyone except me. I've got an artist mom who lives in Rome, Italy. She might be famous— it's hard to tell from her letters—but she's definitely not at home.

Dad looks at me and shakes his head. "Rosita's only a year younger than you. Your friends have got plenty of aunts and uncles. They've got a plan for this."

He turns back to studying the land, and after a while he says, "Everyone has a plan for this."

Usually, when I look out the back porch, I see willows hanging over the creek and red-tail hawks riding the thermals. Today, I see the pasture gate that needs a new hinge, and the south side of the barn that needs paint, and the hayfield that needs mowing, and the tractor that needs a timing belt.

Does he really have a plan for this, the cows and the sheep and the land and me?

I straighten up and measure myself against his shoulder. I've got a ways to go, but my boot's almost as long as his, now that I got a new pair, and I can wear the same work gloves he does. I might be skinny, but I'm big enough to run the tractor and the loader. Lambing and calving? It's bloody, but I know how to do that, too.

"I'm going to take care of this place," I tell him. "It's going to be here. It's going to be just the way you remember it when you get back."

That's my mission, and I'll see it done.

COW CAMP

AUGUST

The trouble with four-thirty in the morning at our cow camp up in the mountains is not just that it's darn early, it's freezing cold too, even in August. I just want to hide in the bottom of my sleeping bag, but I know better than to make Dad call me twice. I slide down from the top bunk and gasp in a big, chilly breath when my bare feet hit the cabin floor.

John's awake already, and sitting on Pete's empty bunk. He looks an inch taller to me since he got back from basic training in June. Maybe it's just the extra muscles. Now that they both have army haircuts, Jim and John could be twins. They both have Grandpa's nose and Dad's square chin, and we all have Grandma's blue eyes. Frank's still got a mop of red hair. It's all I can see sticking out of the top of his sleeping bag. Jim pokes him a couple times to get him out of bed, and Frank growls at him in a much deeper voice than he used to have.

I shiver into my jeans, boots, and three layers of shirt, and head outside. Dad's standing by the gas lamp on the picnic table, with a towel, a razor, and an empty bowl. There's a sheet of ice on top of the water jug.

"I guess we'll have to wait and shave at home," Dad says.

"I'm not shaving," I mumble, unlatching the food box and rooting around for breakfast. I'm never going to shave, if I can help it. Dad decided Frank's big enough to do it this summer because he's going off to high school in a couple weeks. Between the freezing-cold water and the slightly rusty razors, I thought old Frank was going to bleed to death each and every morning.

Dad gathers an armload of wood from the woodpile next to the horse shed and heads back inside. I balance eggs, steak, and coffee beans in one hand and relatch the box with the other. There's nothing grosser than a raccoon eating half your food and pooping on the other half, so I never forget to lock up the box.

Back in the cabin, Frank is finally up and dressed. Dad fusses with the woodstove and then slides the cast-iron skillet into place. I pull up a stool to the long table in the middle of the room, put a couple handfuls of beans into the coffee grinder, and start cranking. John clears away the cards and poker chips from last night and sets the table. Jim is the oldest brother here, so he heads out to the shed to take care of the horses.

I keep thinking one of my brothers is going to say something about Dad leaving today, but I guess not talking is a big tradition nobody told me about up here at cow camp. I've been dying to come every summer since I was nine, when Frank went with the big boys and left me the only kid at home with Grandma. You have to be twelve to go; that's the rule. Dad made an exception this year. I'll be twelve in October, and Dad won't even be back home next summer.

The first orange-pink light from the east window warms up one end of the table. Frank blows out the lamp. Dad puts the last of his Arabic CDs into the player and pops on the headphones while he cooks breakfast. He repeats the same phrases over and over, switching from Arabic to English and back again.

"How many kilometers to the well? The hospital? The police station? The nearest road?"

He turns the steaks over and cracks an egg next to each one.

"Do you need medical help? A translator? Please remain calm. Please clear the area."

He puts two shakes of salt and pepper on each egg and turns it over.

His voice sounds so strange to me in Arabic. His words are stiff and formal, and when I hear them, I feel like he's gone already.

As soon as the steak and eggs smell done, the rest of the brothers are at the table like a shot. I don't even have to call them. Somebody should say something about Dad going. He and I are going to ride back home this morning and then drive to the airport this evening to send off his unit. Fourteen hours and he'll be in the air. But the brothers just pull up their chairs, speed through table grace, and start eating like today is the same as every other day.

Dad's no help either. He goes over the plan of the day with Jim. They drone on about where to move the cows for the best pasture. John and Frank just nod along with the rhythm of Dad's voice as he goes through the list of things to be careful about.

When I was little and my brothers got to bragging about cow camp, they always talked about the jokes they played on each other and the singing at night and the time the bishop came up to bless our cattle. This year it's different. Frank did play a couple jokes on me, but nobody laughed much, and we didn't sing at night, not once. Dad played his harmonica a little bit, but most evenings we sat looking at the fire or playing cards while Dad listened to his language tapes or made up lists and plans.

"Ready to ride home, Brother?"

Dad breaks into my thoughts. I nod, take a last gulp of coffee, and dump my dishes in the dishpan. The brothers head out the door. Dad washes up the plates and pots. I stuff the last of my dirty clothes, three paperbacks, and a book light into my school backpack and head outside.

Jim is under the cluster of mountain larch by the horse shed. He has already got Dad's horse, Ike, saddled. Ike's tall for a quarter horse, and he's probably got some Kiger mustang in him, because he's got a dark stripe down his back and an attitude. He's as good a working horse as we've ever had on the ranch, but he doesn't think much of me.

Spud's my horse. She's just a Shetland pony. I've been riding her since I was four. I'll probably be too tall to ride her next year. Still, I'm glad she's with me now. She might not be fast, but she's plenty strong, and she'd never let me fall. I stroke her head while Jim tightens the saddle girth. She doesn't like that part. When it's done, she nudges me on the shoulder and gives me horse kisses on my neck.

"Listen, Brother," Jim says, throwing an arm over my shoulder and steering me toward the clearing in front of the cabin. "Grandma's going to need lots of extra hugs, with Dad gone. You take good care of her."

Must be an oldest-brother thing to say, because Pete said exactly the same thing to me three weeks ago when his leave was up and he went back to his platoon at Fort Hood.

"I want you to call me right away if something happens," Jim goes on.

I nod.

"Call me even if I'm in class. Boise's not that far away. I could be home in an hour and a half."

"But Dad said no cutting class to do ranch work. Jeez, he said it like a hundred times, remember? The hired man is supposed to do Dad's work."

"I know. I don't mean if something happens on the ranch. I mean if the Grands get sick or . . . you know . . . if something happens with Dad."

I let go of Spud's reins and hide my head in Jim's shoulder, because I've been wanting to talk about that for weeks now. The trouble is, there's nothing to say. He'll either be okay or he won't.

And then Dad comes out of the cabin and ties his gear to the back of the saddle. The boys crowd around him to say goodbye. Dad hugs them and whispers something to each one, and then he stands them up straight. He looks at them as if they are horses he's going to buy, like he wants to memorize every inch of them. Jim and John give him their salutes, and then Dad walks away without a single tear. I don't believe it.

I duck behind Spud so Dad won't see me cry, and then—thank God!—Frank runs over and hugs me up off the ground and shakes me like a dog with a chew toy.

"See ya, Brother! Don't do anything stupid while we're gone."

I wiggle out of his grasp, knock his hat off, and give him an elbow punch in the stomach. "Don't worry about me. You just try not to cut your head off with that razor in the morning."

John's right behind Frank. He puts me in a head-lock and rubs a bunch of tangles into my hair. "Get a haircut, Scruffy!" he says for the thousandth time this summer. Just because his ROTC commander makes him get a military haircut, I don't see why I have to get one. I toss him a few punches, and then the brothers head off to the barn to saddle up their own horses.

I get up on Spud and start down the trail. Dad just sits there on Ike, looking down the mountains past Strawberry Lake to the high desert flats beyond. If there wasn't the haze, you could see the Red Rock Reservoir at the north end of our ranch, thirty miles away.

"Dad?" I say, looking over my shoulder. It's not like him to dawdle when there's a full day of work ahead.

"Do you smell that, Brother?" Dad says.

I take a sniff, but I don't smell anything special.

"That's the smell of your home. That's something you are going to want to take with you when you leave us."

He gives Ike a nudge with his knee, and we head down the trail. I take a couple more sniffs, but I still don't smell anything but air.

We put a few miles behind us before we find some of our cattle in a meadow just up from Strawberry Lake. There's about two dozen red-and-white Herefords and their calves, bunched up in two groups. Dad and I move in to look them over. We've been finding pinkeye in some of the calves, so Dad brought the medicine along. I ride around the near group, and Dad takes the other. I look in both sides of each white face. Sometimes I have to shout and wave my coil of rope to get one of the cows to turn her head. My group's all clear, and I'm glad of it. A cow doesn't like eyedrops any more than I do.

Dad takes one last look at the cows and then checks the ground to make sure they aren't tearing it up too bad. There's about a week's good pasture left, so we move on.

It starts warming up after we get out of the heights. I peel off a shirt. Dad rides behind me, thinking his own thoughts, not talking to me. He's been like this all month. Every minute he's not working the land, he's doing some army paperwork or learning Arabic. Sometimes, even when I'm talking to him, it feels like he's already on the other side of the planet. I have a million things I want to say. I don't even know how to start.

About a mile further on, we hit the steepest part of the trail and the last open spot of mountain pasture. This meadow has Black Angus, and they are more spread out than the Herefords were. Right away I can tell there's a problem, because I can hear a calf crying from somewhere, but I can't see a calf that isn't mothered up. I ride slowly around the meadow, looking under clusters of huckleberry bushes and around boulders where a cow might hide her calf right after birth. I don't see anything, and Dad is hanging back, so I guess he wants me to figure this one out on my own.

I look the cows over again, and there's one with her udder nearly down to the ground. She hasn't been suckled in hours. I give Spud a nudge, and we go take a look at her. She's standing by a long line of boulders where the meadow drops off to a gully that was a creek in the spring, but now it's just a dry wash. I peek over the edge, and there's the calf standing in the rock-strewn gully, bawling. If she's been down there all morning, she's dehydrated and exhausted by now.

No way am I tall enough to lift her up over the rocks. About a hundred yards downhill, there's a gap where I can get Spud and me down in the wash and walk the calf out. I look back at Dad, but he doesn't even nod. I guess this really is my call.

I work Spud down into the dry creek bed. Good thing she's small and steady, because it's really narrow and rocky in there, and hot with the noonday sun. We get about halfway to the calf when Spud starts acting up. She stops, backs up a few steps, and tosses her head like she's trying to look at me and say, "Whose stupid idea was it to ride up this gully?"

I hate when she acts up and Dad's watching. I talk smooth to her and give her a little slap on the butt with my rope, and then she moves clear up to the edge of the higher bank so that blackberry branches snag on my shirt and break off and stick to my jeans.

"Hey, Spud, no fair!" I growl at her. Still, she's moving, so I don't complain too much. We come up on the calf, and she shies away from us. Good thing there's nowhere for her to run. She's a scrawny thing, maybe only a few days old. I toss a loop over her head, thankful I don't have to rope this calf from a run because the truth is, I'm not much good at roping. I tie her off to my saddle horn, tell Spud to stay, and walk over to check her. She's really dirty, and she has cuts and bruises from her fall. I feel her leg bones all the way down, and they're sound.

"Come on, baby. Let's go find your mama." I give the rope a tug, and the calf stretches her neck forward but she doesn't move.

"Come on now. Mama's waiting." I walk behind her and give her a shove from the back like a cow does when she wants her calf to move along. I give her a couple more shoves, and the calf starts walking.

"That's the way, baby." I pull on the rope, and she follows me step by step. I get back in the saddle. We ride nice and slow down the wash, with the calf a few steps behind, until we are at the spot where Spud brushed me against the blackberries. Only this time, Spud stops dead and puts back her ears.

This is not a good sign. I love Spud, but she has her stubborn moments.

"Come on. Let's go. Git up now," I say.

Then I lose my temper and kick her. Spud just snorts, and I am about to kick her again when something about the way she's breathing makes me think she's afraid. I look up at the sky for a thunderhead and along the rim of the gully for cougars. Suddenly, from the ground, I hear the faintest shiver of dry grass in the still air. Before I can even look, Spud rears up and kicks. She bucks me right off. My hat and rope go flying. I come down flat on my back. All the air whooshes out of my lungs. My head is ringing. I still hear the swoosh, and in a second I can see it—a rattlesnake zigzagging through the dead grass, straight at my face.

I am dying to jump up and run, to scream, to breathe. Spud rears up again and tramples the snake with her front feet. I hear a hiss and a faint rattle—the snake is still moving. Just as I finally pull in a ragged, dusty breath, Dad jumps into the gully between me and the snake with his Colt .45 drawn. He takes aim, but doesn't need to fire. The snake is broken in the middle. It drops its head, struggles to lift it again, and uncoils. A dark line of snake blood rolls downhill in the dust.

"You all right, Brother?" Dad holsters his gun.

I nod, even though I've never felt worse in my life. Dad goes after the calf, and I get on my feet and look after my horse. She's a little spooked, and sweaty. I'm glad I'm not the only one. I give her plenty of strokes and soft talk, and when I look up, Dad's standing there with the calf, waiting for me.

He looks me over for a minute and says, "You're going to be more bruises than body come morning. There's nothing worse than coming off a horse onto rocks. Did you break anything?"

I shake my head, and he puts a hand on my shoulder. "Are you ready to ride on?"

As soon as Dad touches me, my whole body starts shaking like a leaf. "I've been scared of snakes for a while, but I guess it's going to be a permanent thing after this."

"A healthy fear of snakes won't bring you to harm. Might do you some good, if you decide to stick with ranch work."

I try to smile, but I'm still shaking.

"You don't have to be brave," he says, real quiet. "Neither of us does. A man's life is not so much about courage. You just have to keep going. You have to do what you've promised, brave or not."

"But I don't want you to go, Dad," I whisper, and then I hug him as hard as I can and say it over and over: "Don't go, Dad. Don't. Don't go."

And Dad hugs me, and he says nothing, but I can feel him cry.

FIRST FLOCK

OCTOBER

"Good game," Grandpa says, and he stands up from the kitchen table to shake my hand.

I say "Good game" back, just out of habit. It's our usual Sunday night chess game, and I still haven't found a way to beat him.

Nobody ever beats Grandpa. My brothers don't even play chess with him anymore. Dad beats him once in a while, but Dad's been in Iraq for two months and sixteen days. Grandpa goes to the shelf by the wood-stove in the living room and reaches down the felt-lined cigar box that holds the chessmen. We lay them in, ebony on one side and ivory on the other because you wouldn't want the troops to mingle and then have to kill each other the next day, would you? It would be bad for morale.

Grandma's got four lamb bottles and a fresh light-bulb waiting for me. She holds up my barn coat and I slide it on, catching a draft of molasses cookies from the left front pocket. I get a wink and a little shove in the direction of the door. Grandma understands about playing chess with Grandpa. I guess she loves all her grandsons the same, but when it comes to chess, it's me she's rooting for. She's got a whole stack of big sisters, so she always says, "Brother, us youngests ought to stick up for each other."

Daylight is still hanging over the Strawberry Mountains, but it's dark enough to see Jupiter two fists up from the barn roof. I hear music coming from the hired-man shack. It sounds magical and sad, like something elves would play. Ernesto plays his pipes in the evening sometimes. When he first came, in September, I loved to hear him play. Now I know he only plays on nights when the letter from his kids in Ecuador is late. Usually a letter comes once a week. Every Friday afternoon, when Grandma comes home from her two hours at the little post office in town, Ernesto is waiting, with his hat in hand like it's a sacred moment.

I know just how he feels, because I hardly ever have a letter from Dad. I know it's a command thing. Battalion commanders are too busy to write. Still, I'm glad it's not my job to tell Ernesto there's no mail from home.

I slide back the barn door and walk past the stalls in the dark, heading for the warm glow of the lamb crib. I climb over the rails and hop in. A mound of pearl white peeks out of the hay, and I count four noses. They're the bum lambs. That's what you call it when the ewe dies and leaves a baby. It hardly seems fair. Being an orphan is depressing enough without being called a bum too. If I can keep these lambs alive all winter, I'll tag them in the spring and keep them in my own flock.

I kick the straw around a bit to find a spot that hasn't been pooped on and settle cross-legged in the corner of the pen, leaning back against a hay bale. The lambs aren't supposed to have names—only horses and dogs are allowed to have names—but I call them Frodo, Merry, Pippin, and Bilbo. I know better than to call one Sam, because Sam is my favorite Hobbit in the whole story.

I pull Pippin into my lap. "Drink up now. I want to see some muscle on these ribs."

Pippin makes a dive for the nipple. Lambs are the sloppiest drinkers. They jerk their heads around and dribble. I shift Pip to the right so I don't get milk drool in my cookie pocket. I wish there were more than four lambs, because they'd keep warmer in the huddle. It's going to get cold tonight.

When Pippin's done I tuck him under my knees, but he's got other ideas. He runs in circles for a bit and then starts jumping up on the hay bale and butting his head on the top rail of the lamb crib. Frodo's all for running around too, so I have to hold him snug to get him to drink his formula.

Frodo has definitely gained a little, but Merry's got a rattle in his breathing. I lift him up and press my ear to his ribs. It's not my imagination. He's got some kind of gunk in his lungs. If he's sick, I should keep him away from the other three, only he'll freeze alone and the others need him for warmth.

I hate this part of ranching. It's way worse than losing at chess. Animals die, and it feels the same amount of awful every time.

By the time I'm done feeding Merry and Bilbo, Pippin is tired again. He flops down in the hay, and the rest of the lambs pile in on top of him. I settle Merry in the heap with his nose pointing toward the other lambs' tails. I put a fresh bulb in the heat lamp and pull it low over them. It's probably not enough. I hop out of the crib and get the bottle of holy water that sits over the barn door. Grandma uses it for the lambing and calving season. She never said I couldn't have some. Grandpa doesn't really hold with holy water and praying to the saints, but he lets Grandma steer the religion around here. I flip up the plastic spout, shake a drop or two on Merry's head, and say Saint Patrick's blessing:

"Christ in front of me. Christ behind me.
Christ on my right side and Christ on my left.
Christ when I go to sleep at night.
Christ wake me up again."

I think about those cougar tracks Grandpa saw yesterday in the hills behind our ranch.

"Christ in every eye that sees me.
Christ in every ear that hears me."

I trace a cross on Merry's head and then cover him up the best I can with straw. I put the holy water back and slip outside.

It's wall-to-wall stars now, with nothing to block the view except the empty branches of the big cottonwood. I lean on the barn door and look up. The Herdsman constellation ought to be rising over by the notches of rock where Starvation Creek cuts through. The bottom half of him is still behind the hills at the north side of our land. I stay to watch him rise, because he's the constellation Dad and me picked to watch over me while he's gone. A second later, I change my mind because it's getting really cold. I pull out my cookie and head for the house.

Grandpa is finishing up with the sheep. He keeps a gun pretty close when there are cougars around. I don't want him to think I'm sneaking up on him. He'd probably shoot first and check species second. I belt out some Alleluias, spraying cookie crumbs all the way up to the house.

I reckon my grandpa's the only Quaker member of the National Rifle Association. He's a dead-serious pacifist and the best marksman around. He's gotten coyotes, cougars, and even a full-grown bear. No trophy antlers cluttering up our parlor, though. It's not the Quaker way to shoot a vegetarian.

It's too bad. Over at the VFW, they make a venison stew that gets me begging for seconds before the bowl's even half empty. We spend a lot of time over at the VFW because Grandma is a veteran of foreign wars. She drove some general in a jeep all over France in the

Second World War, and as if that wasn't enough, she maintained the Army Reserve motor pool for about a hundred years. She's got a scrapbook full of pictures and maps and signatures of famous people she's met. The one that's framed and hanging on the wall at the VFW meeting hall is when her general met General Eisenhower right after the Battle of the Bulge. Grandma's the one holding three briefcases, a shoebox-sized radio, and a thermos of coffee. She's tall as any man, with curly red hair and a movie star smile.

Grandpa hates that picture. "That's no way to treat a lady," he says.

Grandma just laughs. "That's exactly the way to treat a corporal."

It's my favorite picture because it's plain to see: those generals were winning because Grandma had them all working like a fine-tuned tractor. There's not a machine on our ranch that would dare drop a bolt while Grandma's around. She's got hands like a basketball player, and when she lifts up the hood, well, any truck in its right mind would know she means business.

The light from the kitchen window makes a square pool of yellow in the front yard, and the shadow from the flag by the front door makes a ghost shape when a gust of air hits it. I walk up the front steps and slam the door quick to keep the warm air in. I slump down on the bench in the front hall, pull off my boots, and hang my coat on the peg between Frank's and Dad's.

In the kitchen, I leave the empty lamb bottles in the sink. Grandma sits on her rolling stool by the computer and orders cow vaccines online. I pull up a chair at the kitchen table and unwrinkle my fractions homework.

Grandpa comes in last. I can hear the thump of him taking off his work boots in the front hall. He walks around the corner into the kitchen, leans over to kiss Grandma, and then warms his hands on the china coffeepot before refilling Grandma's mug.

"Second dinner, Brother? Plenty of stew in the pot," he says.

Actually, it'll make third dinner for me tonight, but who's counting?

"Mhmm," I say. I get up and bring a bowl to the stove. "Don't you want any, Grandpa?"

"No thanks."

I fill up my bowl and get back to my homework while Grandpa takes out his journal and sits in the easy chair by the woodstove. Deep quiet settles around us. It's too cold for bug noises and too calm for wind noises. Sometimes it gets so quiet at night, I'd swear you can hear the stars twinkle.

Grandma finishes up her computer business and spins around on her stool. "There's an e-mail waiting for you. Are you done with that math?"

I give a yes grunt, rewrinkle the page, and tuck it down in the bottom of my backpack, where the wrinkles will get pressed in good. I know I've got them all right, but it's best to keep up appearances.

Grandma doesn't say who it's from. She just goes into the living room with Grandpa to sit in the recliners and watch the news. I try not to care if it's from Dad. I cross my fingers under the table as I click the envelope on the screen.

It's just the Sunday night e-mail from Frank. Maybe he knows what to do for lamb cough. Dad can cure any animal he sets a hand on, but it's not fair to worry him about ranch stuff when he can't do anything to help. Grandpa sends him a weekly update with all the good news. If there's bad news, he just says *The weather's about right for the time of year* or *Beef prices are about what we were thinking they'd be.*

I bet Dad sees right through Grandpa's messages. Still, a rule's a rule. If I'm going to get advice, it's going to have to be my brothers.

Probably Frank will just tell me something depressing like *Half of all bum lambs die in their first week, and a bunch more don't make it past a month. Just don't get too attached.* I know he's right. Nobody fusses about death except me. They always shrug and say "That's life," in exactly the same tone of voice that they say "That's baseball" when I strike out.

The thing is, I hate striking out and I hate death. I hate it every time. Nobody teases me when I get all sad, but I see them shake their heads at each other like they're wondering, How am I ever going to be a real rancher? And what else am I going to be? Ranching and soldiering is what men do around here.

Frank's e-mail is the usual boring gripes about too much homework and the usual annoying questions about how the Grands are doing. Does he think Grandpa's going to forget how to run a ranch after doing it for fifty years? I give him the usual yeah-everything's-fine so he can go back to his usual I've-got-everything-under-control frame of mind. It's not like he can help me from a high school dorm room fifty miles away.

Besides, I remember what I really need. I head down the hall to Dad's bedroom and open the nightstand drawer. There's a big bottle of Advil in there, and a tube of Ben-Gay, his wedding ring, the harmonica, a bunch of pictures, and underneath that a black leather book. The cover is scratched and the edges curl. It's labeled RECIPES, REMEDIES, FORMULAS. The main part is in my great-grandpa's curvy writing. Some of the really old remedies are written in Irish. There are some remedies in Grandma's tidy cursive, and toward the end, Dad wrote a few new formulas. I find what I need between the recipes for glue and house paint.

I read it twice to memorize it and head back toward the kitchen. Grandma's asleep in her recliner, but Grandpa's still awake, mending a bridle and frowning over the weather report. I tell him my plan and right away I can see he doesn't like it, but he just bobs his head up and down and says nothing. Grandma says it's a Quaker thing to think before you speak. You wouldn't catch any of the Irish in the family doing it.

"You will take the big flashlight, be back in twenty minutes, and wear your woolies."

I hate my woolies.

"Yes, Grandpa."

I'm such a liar. Grandpa will be asleep by the time the medicine is cooked. He'll never know I went out without my wool underwear.

The recipe's pretty easy, but I measure everything level and time the boiling so it's perfect. Outside, the stars are gone and the clouds are low. I sprint for the barn. The squeak of the door is swallowed by cold night air.

The heat lamp makes a yellow circle of warmth in the corner of the barn. I cozy up to the light and lift Merry's head to drink. At first he doesn't want any, but once he gets a taste of it, he's slurping it down like a drunken sailor.

Pippin wakes up and starts calling for his mama. He can hear the rest of the sheep outside, and I bet he thinks she's still out there, looking for him. I try my best to make a mama-sheep sound for him. After a while, Pippin quiets down and comes close, where I can stroke him.

"*¡Hola!*" a deep voice barks from the door. "Who there?"

I hear a rifle being cocked.

"No!" I shout, diving over the lambs and trying to tuck their heads and legs under my body.

"Ignacio?"

It's Ernesto. I'm so relieved I could throw up. He walks over, and suddenly it seems silly to have dived over my lambs like we are soldiers in a foxhole. Who else would be clear out here in the middle of the night? At the edge of the lamplight, all I can see are his boots.

"Medicine?" Ernesto asks, nodding at the bottle.

"*Sí.*"

"Cough?"

"*Sí.*"

He leans over the rail and rests a broad, callused hand on my shoulder. "Heart of a shepherd," he says, like he's pronouncing a blessing. Then the boots turn, and I hear him walk out to the sheep pens to check for more newborn lambs.

It's a funny thing to say. Sons grow up to be ranchers. Shepherds come from South America. But I like the way he said it.

I stroke Merry's chest while he drinks. Pippin falls asleep with his chin on my knee, and my head is bobbing by the time the bottle's empty. I trudge up to the house. Grandma is still asleep, glasses way down on her nose and a book of poetry sliding off her knees. Grandpa is snoring steadily. So I turn off the news and haul myself into bed.

"Heart of a shepherd." I try it out a few times as

I'm putting on pajamas. It has a solid ring to it, like Purple Heart or Medal of Honor. I've read all the dragon books on my shelf, so I tiptoe down the hall to Jim and John's room and hunt up something with sailing ships to read myself to sleep.

The first thing I see in the morning is snow on the hills. Yes! The best part of going to a two-room school is that we get to go sledding for PE.

Grandpa is already heading into the winter pasture with a load of hay for the cows. I hustle into my clothes and pick up an armload of lamb bottles on my way out the door.

The barn door is open a few inches. Weird. Who was in the barn this morning? I'm the one who goes in there first thing. I slide the door open a little wider. Did I close it last night? I search my memory. Damnation! I run to the lamb crib.

Gone. Pippin is gone. I look all over the barn for him, but it's obvious what happened. The straw is pushed away from the corner of the crib nearest the door, and the bottom board is pushed out.

That feeling I get when something dies grabs me by the throat. I set down the bottles and pull Merry into my lap. I want to say, It's all right, buddy, I'm here.

I'll take care of you. My throat is squeezed so tight, I can't get a word out. I stroke his knobby little head and pick up the bottle. Merry dives for it and starts gurgling it down. I can still feel that rattle in his breathing, but it doesn't seem so bad. He's not leaking goop out of his eyes or ears, either. That's a good sign. The squeeze in my throat eases up just enough for me to breathe steady. Now I'm mad.

"All right, God," I say, tucking Frodo in for his bottle. "This is not making you look good. It's not like I'm asking you to look after a hundred sheep here. I just wanted your help with these four. Plus, I'm not asking you about ostriches or llamas or some animal you never heard of. Sheep are in the Bible, you know."

Ernesto comes in and goes to the workbench to strap on a carpenter's belt. He sticks in a hammer and a handful of nails, and pulls on work gloves.

"*¿Dónde está la otra oveja?*" he asks, leaning on the top rail.

I try to explain, but that catch in my throat holds the words back. I point to the loose board. He kneels and pushes the board back in place. His frown makes him look old.

"I fix," he says. For some reason, seeing Ernesto sad makes me feel better.

"Maybe he's still out there."

Ernesto shakes his head, still frowning.

"You to school. I to find."

"But he knows me. I could call him." I can hear how stupid this sounds. You can't call sheep. They just don't come.

"I look. I find."

I swallow that worried lump down into my stomach. I put on half a smile, say *"Gracias,"* and trudge up the porch steps. I bet there's not even enough snow for sledding.

School drags on for centuries. I coast through the whole explanation of decimals. I keep looking out the window, thinking about wolves and coyotes and that cougar up on the ridge. I head for the computer lab on the girls' side of the room for online Spanish. I don't even bother to tug on Rosita's braid or dump glitter in the hood of her sweatshirt on the way over, even though she's been sitting right across from me, making faces all morning.

After a few minutes, she comes and works at the computer beside me. "Hey, Brother, what's the matter? Mom and Dad called me last night. Nothing bad has happened lately."

I just shrug and look away.

"Really, they would have said if something happened to your dad."

"It's nothing," I mumble, and turn my chair away from her.

She flicks bits of chalk at me to cheer me up.

It doesn't help.

I settle in for online Spanish and an e-mail pops up. It's from Dad! I ditch the Spanish and pull up his message.

From: col-alderman@army.mil.gov
To: ignatius-alderman@redrockvalley.k12.or.us
Son,

I'm going to be away from phones all week, so I'm going to miss your birthday. Sorry about that, but I want to know, what's really going on at home? Is everyone healthy? Any problems with the stock? How's Ernesto working out? Thanks for all your hard work.

Love,
Dad

His e-mails are all like this, ever since he landed in Iraq. It's like he's briefing a general or something. I read it over four times, in case there's a secret code in it. I'm dying to tell Dad about Pippin. He knows what it's like.

He used to raise the bum lambs when he was a kid. And he's the one person who really gets it when I'm upset about the animals. He always used to take me for a walk up by the reservoir to look at the stars, and he'd put his heavy arm over my shoulder and say, "Brother, if it was one of my soldiers, I'd feel exactly the same way." Sometimes he'd ask me to pray for some soldier of his who was becoming a new father or taking a tough exam, and we'd pray with a nice stretch of silence. And then I'd ask him to pray for one of my animals, or for all the animals not fast enough to outrun a wildfire. He would pray just as long for animals as people.

Sometimes he'd tell me the myths that go with the constellations, or we'd talk about who was a better general, Odysseus or Patton. I imagine Dad all gritty and sweating in a truck somewhere in the Iraqi desert, praying for his soldiers, all alone. I count backward on my fingers. It's an hour after midnight out there. I hope he has stars to look at.

From: ignatius-alderman@redrockvalley.k12.or.us
To: col-alderman@army.mil.gov

I love you, Dad.

Everyone's healthy at home. We got a bit of snow last night, so good thing Grandma got the heater on the truck fixed.

Ernesto's great. He doesn't let Grandpa lift any of the heavy things. He was good at the lambing last week, very clean, and he's nice to me. The stock is all fine. About where you'd expect them to be this time of year. Be careful, Dad. I miss you.

Brother

I hit *Send* fast, before I think of what I really want to say.

Rosita stares at me with those serious brown eyes like she knows exactly what I'm thinking. Girls are so nosy. I nibble off my eraser and flick it at her to prove I'm fine.

When the bell finally rings, I'm on the school bus first. Paco sits next to me. One thing I like about him: he never bugs me when I don't feel like talking. Fortunately, the bus driver doesn't believe in speed limits. When he hits our driveway, brakes squealing, I don't even wait for the little red sign to pop out. I jump down the steps and push the door open myself. The driver waves to Grandma, working on the tractor by the corral, and then backs the bus out to the road to turn it around.

Ernesto is walking up from the creek. It's not a happy walk.

"Did you find my lamb?"

He nods. No smile. I quick-check his hands and clothes for blood. Nothing.

"Is he dead?"

"*Sí.*"

"Was it wolves? The cougar?"

Ernesto shakes his head. "*No lobos, no puma.* Cold."

There isn't really anything to say. We stand there for a bit, looking at the gravel driveway, making breath-smoke in the cold air. Ernesto reaches into his pocket and pulls out his pipes. He holds them out to me. They look like a row of thick wooden straws tied together.

"For you," he says. "To lift up."

I shake my head. "That's for you and your *niños.* You must miss them."

"I must work for them. This"—he holds his pipes close—"this is good for my heart. And you, you miss your papa?" He looks away from me so I know I don't have to say anything if I don't want to. "What is good for your heart?"

"I dunno. I don't really think about it, I guess."

Ernesto puts his pipes back in his pocket and goes to the sheep pens, and I head for the house.

"More lambs today?" I call after him.

"More lambs, one week."

That's life, I guess. I dump my backpack in the kitchen and go down the hall to Dad's room. We are going to lose lambs every year, and I don't know how to not care.

I open Dad's nightstand drawer and pull out the harmonica. I shine it up a bit on the edge of my sweatshirt. I don't know how to play it, but just the shape of it in my hand makes me feel better. I slip it into my pocket, just in case it turns out to be good for my heart, and head out to take care of my flock.

THE MAN OF THE HOUSE

DECEMBER

If animals could really talk on Christmas Eve, like they do in all the legends, they'd be saying, "What the heck are you still doing in the barn? Your chores are already done, kid."

Dad's horse, Ike, shakes his big head at me as I go back and forth with the push broom. Patton and Bradley, our cutting horses, make worried snorts as they watch me hide all the unfinished fix-it-up jobs on the workbench. I've been at the barn chores an hour longer than Grandpa, and the extra sweeping works open a tear in my leather glove. Cold air whispers across my palm. I walk over to the bare lightbulb by the barn door. The rip is straight down, from my thumb to the wrist, just like the one I got in the other glove last month. Grandpa will help me stitch it up. He used to be an army medic, so he does all the stitching around here, clothes and injured animals, too. I fish around in the workbench drawer for the roll of green army duct tape. It's not pretty, but it will keep me from getting a blister while I haul the last of the muck out of the barn. I should probably sweep up the sawdust and get the wood scraps out to the woodpile. Custer, the barn cat, weaves himself between my legs and looks up at me like I'm a crazy person.

I can't help it. All my brothers will be here tonight, and I just want them to see that Grandpa and I are doing things right; we aren't too old or too young. I want to show them that I'm putting in a man's day even though I'm a full-time sixth grader.

I hear Grandma's truck pull into the driveway, so I run out to see my brothers. Frozen mud-ripples crunch under my boots, and breath-smoke trails behind me. In a second, I am in the swarm of my brothers, and each one has a go at cracking my ribs with a big bear hug. Pete's carrying a box with stamps from Italy, my Christmas box from Mom. It'll be the same as always, I bet— a sweater in a color I wouldn't wear if you held a gun to my head, and a big stack of the coolest books ever.

Grandma sweeps us all up the front porch, with the good smell of roast beef, biscuits, and apple pie helping us along.

She stops at the flag by the front door, like she has every day since Dad left for Iraq, to give it a stroke and whisper a prayer for him. The rest of the brothers pile into the kitchen while I lurk in the front hall and watch her. There are lumps of ice all along the edge of the flag. She slips off her gloves and cups her hands around the frozen edge, blowing to melt it. My mind zooms to Dad out in the gritty ghettos of Baghdad, where Christmas is just another day and nobody will touch him gentle like Grandma would. I can't think about him alone on Christmas. I won't. He wouldn't even want me to. Grandma lets the melted flag go, and I duck into the kitchen so she won't know I watched.

The brothers are all stomping around, giving each other directions on how to set the table, like this is somehow tricky and needs a four-man consultation. The house seems small with all of them in it, and I feel like the little kid I used to be when they all lived at home.

Once dinner is ready, Grandma gets the Baby Jesus figure. We all follow her as she carries it to the Nativity scene on the mantel, and we sing "O Come,

All Ye Faithful." Then we stand around the table and sing some more carols. I love it when we sing together, but the brothers can't carry a tune in a bucket. Grandpa has a great voice, but he just doesn't sing out the Hosannas with the same gusto Dad does. Musically, we are in deep trouble without him. Nobody even complains when we cut the singing short and get down to the business of eating.

Usually Grandma runs the conversation at dinner, but she's quiet today, and the brothers work through the beef, potatoes, gravy, biscuits, and cranberry sauce with silent devotion. Grandpa's hand shakes a little, like it does sometimes at the end of the day, and he hardly eats, which is nuts, because he works harder than me, and I'm starving!

Once the boys move into seconds, Grandpa gets news out of them: the weather and the soldiers in Pete's platoon in Texas, Jim and John's final exams at Boise State, and the dorm pranks Frank is in on at the high school. Nobody asks me about my news because everything I'm doing, they've already done. Finally, Pete asks about the lambs, and I mumble that I lost one because we're all being very careful not to say anything about death.

And then Pete says, "Well, how many have you saved?"

"Seven," I admit, because after Frodo, Bilbo, and Merry, there were four more.

"Seven—well, that's a good start. You'll get eight or ten pounds of wool from each one starting in the spring, and if you take good care of them, they should double in a year. You'll have a good-sized flock pretty soon."

"Now, that's a solid start to your college," Grandpa says. "You build yourself a good flock to sell and you won't have to worry about getting one of those army scholarships."

"I guess one of us better plan on staying with the land," Pete says. "If we all go on active duty, who will run the place?"

He sounds so much like Dad when he says this that I'm just itching to kick him under the table. It's bad enough that no one thinks I'm much of a rancher; since when am I not good enough to be in the army? I'm not going to be this short forever.

"What do you want to study?" Grandma says, passing around third helpings.

I just shrug and rearrange the potatoes on my plate.

"Dude, don't go for engineering. No girls," John says. "And don't become a teacher either, because those classes are just packed with bossy girls."

"The army likes engineering grads," Jim says. "They pretty much get their pick of which branch they want to sign up with."

And then we are onto the topic of what branch of the army Jim will go into when he graduates next year, and I get to thinking about the long line of soldiers that have marched away from this table, which is great if you're the patriotic type. But it's not so great if you are the one waiting for your dad to come home.

After dinner is the best part of Christmas Eve. Grandpa gets out our favorite Monty Python movie, and us boys drag our pillows and blankets off the bunks and out to the floor under the Christmas tree. We laugh at all the stupid parts and say all the good lines and act out the fights, including catapulting our old teddy bears over the tree and down the hall. Traditionally, Grandma does the dishes while we watch, saying "Outrageous!" and "Blasphemy!" every ten minutes, and sounding more Irish as the movie goes on.

But this year Grandma just leaves the dishes in the sink and goes to bed, and Grandpa actually falls asleep in his recliner before we get to the killer-rabbit part.

Pete turns the volume down and shushes us about saying the lines, and suddenly it's not such a funny movie when everyone is behaving.

"Come on," Jim says. "Let's get those dishes. It's a lot of work to have guests. God knows, the Grands don't need extra work."

"Guests?" Frank says, trailing us into the kitchen. "We aren't guests; we live here."

I've got nothing to say about this because I'm the only one who lives here now, which gets real obvious when I'm the only person who remembers where the soap and clean dish towels are.

"All right, men," Pete says, putting on his command voice. "I'll scrub; John can dry and put away. Jim, clear the table and counters, and Frank, sweep and mop."

He forgot a job for me. Dad never forgets a job for me.

I'm an inch from turning around and slugging him, but the Nativity on the mantel catches my eye, and something about the Holy Family all snug and together in the stable melts me.

"I guess I'll make everybody hot chocolate," I say, pulling a step stool over to the cupboard. I make killer hot chocolate. I get out the big pot, the cocoa, the sugar, and the milk jug. It's Christmas; maybe I'll make a whole gallon.

Jim launches into another of his "perfect date" stories while we work. Nobody actually believes he's been on a date, but I love the part with the girl, the rope trick, the parking meter, and the awkward conversation with the Boise patrolman. He's just about to launch into another when John says, "Hey, I wonder what Grandma's got in the sinners' cupboard." Pete reaches up and brings down an almost full bottle of Irish whiskey.

What a stupid idea.

"Hey, guys, the hot chocolate is done," I say to distract them. I pour beautiful steaming cocoa into the china coffeepot and line up a row of mugs.

"Excellent!" Pete says, pouring himself half a cup of cocoa and topping it off with whiskey.

Oh, man! It was perfect. It smelled perfect. It was heaven by the spoonful, and he dumped gasoline in it. Jim and John are right behind him, and Frank too— that traitor!

Fine. I take my cup to the far corner of the kitchen and hoard all the whipped cream. I figure the brothers are going to get all rowdy now, so it's weird when they just stand around saying nothing and looking at the half-mopped floor.

"Do you think they are going to send your unit to Iraq anytime soon?" John says, not looking at Pete.

Pete shrugs and takes a slow sip from his cocoa. "Not for a while yet. We're gearing up to train deploying troops for now, but if we're in Iraq for the long haul . . ." He looks at Jim, and then John. "I bet we'll all get our turn out there."

The four of them nod their heads over their hot chocolate and study the ground. It's not like anyone needs to say it, but how are we going to keep the ranch going with everybody gone? Pete pours a second round of whiskey.

Finally, Jim says, "The Grands look so old, all of a sudden."

"Yeah," John says, "and since when does Grandma go to bed at eight o'clock and leave the kitchen a mess?"

"Grandpa doesn't stand up as straight as he used to," Pete adds.

Like bad posture is some kind of moral failure.

"I don't get it," Frank says. "The hired man does all the really heavy work, but Grandpa looks exhausted every time I see him. You know, they only came to one basketball game this year, and it was just down the road, in Vale."

"The cold is hard on him," Pete says. "Look how skinny he's gotten."

Now being skinny is a crime? I scoop up an extra spoonful of whipped cream and drown it in my cocoa.

"Remember when Dad and Grandpa used to take us out on the hay wagon Christmas Eve to look for the Christmas star?"

And then they go on about all the great things that happened at Christmas in their childhood but not in mine, Christmases when Dad and Mom were both home. My gut starts churning, and even the hot chocolate doesn't sweeten me up.

Then conversation switches back to all the things that need doing around the ranch and whether Grandpa will be strong enough to do them. Pete says, in his most annoying trying-to-be-Dad voice, "We should make a plan for what to do, just in case—"

That's it. I can't take another word.

"We're fine!" I shout. "We're doing just fine. It's you—all of you. You're the ones who are gone!"

And then I just can't cry in front of my brothers, so I attack.

I kick Frank in the shins as hard as I can and he falls down, cussing as he goes. He knocks into Jim, so I ram Jim in the gut with my head. Jim trips over Frank and goes down laughing, which makes me even madder. I swing punches at Pete and land some good ones, but he won't even fight back. Then John comes up behind me and scoops me off the floor, pinning my left hand to my ribs. I flail around with my legs and reach for the only weapon I can find, the hot chocolate pot. I grab it and crash it down on Pete's head as hard as I can.

It explodes in my hand.

Frank and Jim start howling as the rest of the hot chocolate rains down on them, and John drops me so I'm standing on Jim's hand. Pete staggers over to the sink, groaning.

"Dude," John almost whispers, "you assaulted an officer, and he's bleeding!"

"Explain this," Grandpa says in a voice that is even more scary because it's calm and comes out of nowhere.

I turn around and there he is, standing in the doorway looking bone-weary, and I am standing in a puddle of brothers and hot chocolate with the broken handle of a coffeepot in my hand and blood on my knuckles.

"Ignatius kicked the shit out of us, Grandpa," Pete says with his back turned. "He did a hell of a job."

Groans of agreement come from the floor.

"Dude," John says again a little louder, "you are really bleeding."

It's true. Still gripping the edge of the sink, Pete lifts his head up. Two rivers of blood roll down either side of his face.

"John," Grandpa says, "my medical kit is in the barn."

John's out the door so fast, he doesn't stop for a coat. Frank and Jim untangle themselves and stagger to their feet. Grandpa walks around the pool of cocoa. He looks from the half-empty bottle of whiskey on the counter to each of us in turn, and that's about all the scolding I need. I feel terrible, and I didn't even touch a drop.

Grandma is not at a loss for words. She starts in on the scolding, full volume from her bedroom at the far end of the hall. "Jesus, Mary, and Joseph! For heaven's sake, boys—brawling on the holiest night of the year! What would your father—Lord help us!"

She comes into the kitchen, and we quick line up, tall to short, because the truth is, we've been in trouble with Grandma before. She looks up the row—from me, still holding the coffeepot handle, past Frank and Jim, to Pete, bleeding down into his collar.

"Angels and saints," she says, not shouting now.

The front door bangs and John dashes in, breathing hard and shivering, with the medical kit in hand.

"Set it by my chair, John," Grandpa says. "I'll wash first. Pete, lean over the sink. Boys, I want all the broken pieces off the floor."

Grandpa washes his hands and then takes Pete's head and rinses it in great bloody gallons of cold water. I shouldn't watch. Blood makes me dizzy, even natural blood from lambing and calving. But there's Grandpa, up to his elbows in it and calm as a summer day. Grandpa sees me watching him and says, "Head wounds bleed a lot. Pete's going to be fine."

I nod.

"Go. Wash your hands twice. Do a good job."

"What?"

"Brother, there are probably little shards of china in this cut, but I can't see them, and I won't be able to pull them out. You are the only man here with a clear eye and a steady hand."

"But I can't—"

"You will."

"But I never—"

"You must."

"Grandpa!"

"I'll teach you."

I wipe my sweaty hands on my chocolate-covered shirt and nod slowly. Grandma has the towels ready by Grandpa's chair. I head down the hall to the bathroom, and a whole chorus of brain waves is chanting that I can't do this. *This is crazy. You can't pretend to be a doctor just because someone needs you—not when you are only a kid.*

I run the water and pump out a big handful of soap. I don't even want to look in the mirror, so I look down at the wet, sticky front of my pajamas. I tug the shirt off with one sudsy hand, dry my hands on the clean side, and kick it behind the bathroom door. The draft from the bathroom window raises a shiver all down my back. I peek down the hall, and no one is looking, so I slip into the dark of Dad's room. I stumble over his clean work boots on my way to the dresser and find his wool flannel work shirt by touch in the drawer. It's blue and brown plaid, and worn thin at the elbows. I wrap it tight around my chest and breathe in the dad smell that is still stuck in the collar.

Dad lets me do stuff. It's just my brothers who think I'm too little.

I let Dad's shirt hang down to my knees and start buttoning. "Piece of cake, Brother," Dad would say to me. "Grandpa's done sutures a million times. It's about time you learned how."

Dad would hug me.

I trail my hand over his pillow on the way out the door. I head back to the living room, and everyone is waiting like an audience. Pete's kneeling by Grandpa's recliner with his head right under the reading lamp. Grandma is sitting in the chair, holding Pete's hands. "Holler all you need to, Pete. There's none but the good Lord and them that love you to hear," she says.

This is not exactly encouraging, but Grandpa smiles at me like stitching up your brother's head is a perfectly normal thing to do.

"Let's take a look," he says.

Before he can lift up the towel over the wound, Pete turns to me and says, "I'm sorry, Brother. You and Grandpa are doing fine, way more than your share."

"Dude, the barn looks perfect," John adds.

Frank nods, and Jim says, "What would we do without you?"

I just open and close my mouth a bunch of times,

so Grandpa says, "Thank you, boys," for me, and hands me the long tweezers with the bent end. I brace myself to be grossed out by the wound. Grandma starts praying the rosary, with the brothers chiming in, but when Grandpa takes the cloth away it's not nearly as bad as I thought it would be. The main thing is, I can't see Pete's face, plus the cut is only about two inches long.

"You want to pull out the shards just like a wood sliver," Grandpa says. "Pull them out the same direction they went in. Can you see them?"

I tilt Pete's head a bit more toward the light. I push his bristle-short black hair apart with my thumbs.

"Yup, I see a big one and two little ones."

"Nice and steady now," Grandpa says.

I slowly, slowly lower the tweezers and get a grip on the shard. Pete sucks in a sharp gasp. Panic starts to creep up my arms and make my hands shake. Pete gasps again, and then groans. Frank sits down suddenly on the floor and puts his head between his knees.

"Breathe," Grandpa says softly. "Everybody breathe. Angels are all around us now. We can do this."

Grandma presses on with the rosary. I shake out my hand and try again. This time I steady my wrist on the top of Pete's head, and it goes much better. Grandpa holds out a saucer for me to put the piece of china on and a teacup full of rubbing alcohol to rinse the tweezers in. The next two shards are easier because they are small and don't make Pete twitchy when I pull them out. I take one last look.

"Let me do this next part," Grandpa says, and he takes gauze dipped in disinfectant and wipes out the wound. Pete takes in a big gasp. Every muscle in his arms and shoulders bunches up.

"Okay, now for the stitching," Grandpa says. He hands me the medium-sized curved needle. I thread a length of black thread on it.

"Remember that stitch I taught you when you were mending your leather gloves? We're going to use the same stitch here, and it will feel a lot the same as working on your glove. Pete's scalp is a bit thinner, but skin is skin."

I am never going to wear leather anything for the rest of my life.

"Okay, start with the end nearest you and take a bite with your needle about a millimeter back from the edge."

I breathe in a big gulp, grit my teeth, and then stick the needle in Pete's head. He squeezes his praying hands together tighter but doesn't make a peep.

"Excellent, now do the same on the opposite side. . . . Perfect, now draw them together. . . . Now the knot." Grandpa walks me through each step.

"Hey! The edges on either side of the thread just joined up and stuck together! Wow, Grandpa, that was the weirdest thing!"

"That's the miracle of healing right there, Brother. We were meant to be whole and healthy."

I snug the knot down tight and move to the next stitch. As I do, I see clear yellowish fluid seep into the margins of the cut and form the shiny shell of a new scar. Amazing.

I chew that idea about healing over good, because ten minutes ago I was trying to kill Pete, and now that he really, really needs me, I've never loved him so much.

I tie off the last knot and blow out a huge breath of relief.

"Beautiful!" Grandpa says, and his warm hand squeezes my shoulder. "Just a dab of this and you'll be done." He hands me a tube of ointment.

"Is it over?" Frank says, still hiding his head.

"He was awesome," Jim says, pulling Frank to his feet.

"Don't worry, we'll make a cowboy of you yet," John says. "You don't even have to put the stitches that close together when it's a cow."

The brothers gather around to inspect my work. I squat down and take a look at Pete. He looks a little gray and his hands are shaky, but he gives me a smile anyway.

"Sleep," Grandma announces briskly. "Growing boys need sleep."

The brothers grumble a little just for effect, and Grandpa puts another log in the woodstove while we settle our blankets under the tree.

Hours later, when the brothers are long past snoring, I've got my head propped on Pete's belly and my feet up on Frank. I keep drifting in and out of sleep, watching the red glow of the fire wave like a flag on the living room wall. When I dream, there are rivers of blood and singing, and when I wake up again I can see how Pete's wound sealed up just like magic. But then I fall asleep and dream of fires and bells, and wake up freezing. The fire is out, but the phone is ringing. Pete sits up and reaches for it on the coffee table.

"Dad?" Pete mumbles. "Dad! Hey, Merry Christmas!"

It's Dad. I'm warm clear to the ends of my fingers.

I start to nudge the brothers awake. Pete is saying, "Yeah, Dad, of course . . . all of us under the Christmas tree. We remembered. . . . Listen, Dad, I think you'd better speak to the man of the house."

And Pete hands the phone straight to me.

SERVING THE ALTAR

FEBRUARY

It's the first Sunday of Lent, the first almost warm day of the year. The last patches of frozen ground have gone mushy, and there are pale green buds on the cottonwood tree on the sunny side of the barn. Grandma lets me drive the truck the first mile to church, but once we are off our own land I get out and sit in the backseat with Ernesto.

"What do you think the new priest will be like?" I ask Grandma after we've switched places.

"Taller."

Grandpa grunts out a laugh, his hands folded over his black leather journal.

"Thanks. Very helpful."

Our last priest, Father Rosetti, was the size of a Hobbit and getting shorter, with the face of an evil dwarf—all north-and-south wrinkles and beady black eyes. If you met him on the street, you would immediately suspect him of poisoning Snow White. But he had a beautiful voice, with a lift at the end of his words like the Italians do. At least I guess they do. Father Rosetti is the only person I've ever met that actually came out of Italy.

I remember him standing on a box to see over the lectern and preaching in his beautiful voice about how having faith is like falling in love. If he hadn't been 112 years old, I would have definitely asked him how he knew about love. Father Rosetti is retired now—or maybe he just got so small they can't find him anymore—so we've got a new priest, a circuit-riding Jesuit named Ziegler.

"He's from New York City," Grandma says. "We'll have him for a year."

It's hard to get a priest in a little country parish like ours because they don't want to live out here, so the bishop checks one out to us like a library book. The priest rides the circuit of three parishes, sixty miles apart. We've never had a priest stay with us more than two and a half years. What we need is a priest who grew up around here and wants to stay, somebody who understands how people who live off the land pray.

We get to church half an hour before everyone else because Grandma has the keys and pretty much runs the show here at Sacred Heart. We climb out of the truck, and Ernesto takes the coffee cakes and doughnuts over to the parish hall for after Mass.

There's already a car in the lot. It's a hybrid.

"This is fancy," Grandpa says. To him, "fancy" is practically a swear.

Grandma shushes him with a flap of her hand because there's the new priest, sitting on the church steps, in jeans, city shoes, and a businessman's shirt. He is tall and thin, and a bit pale for these parts.

"You're early," Grandma says.

He stands up, smiling, and when he says good morning it's in an accent I've never heard in my life, so it must be a New York City accent. "I gave myself some extra time. I haven't driven a car in years. There was never a need when I lived in New York."

That remark meets with dead silence, since it's practically the same as admitting you forgot how to tie your own shoes.

"So did you have trouble finding our church?" I offer after we've all spent a few moments digesting his lack of driving experience.

"No, it was easy. There's pretty much just the one road."

This is not true, but it occurs to me that none of the other roads around here are on the map, and maybe this guy is expecting us all to show up in donkey carts.

Grandma tells him our names and he says his name is Father Ziegler, and after a bit of the usual grown-up chitchat Grandma unlocks the door. I carry the altar cloth Grandma ironed last night up to the front of the church.

Grandma goes over to the Mary statue. She puts fresh candles in the stand and then gives Mary a little kiss on the toes, which seems weird to me even though I know it's a normal devotion and Grandma's probably done it every Sunday of her life. I asked her about it a while back, and she said that once you have babies, you kind of fall into the habit of toe-kissing, and then it seems like an ordinary thing to do. But seriously, now that I know about the toe-kissing thing, I'm absolutely not becoming a dad, because what are the odds that it's the only gross habit you pick up from babies?

Father Ziegler just stands there looking around the

church, and I wonder if he's thinking, Where the heck did the bishop send me this time? I bet he's used to a tall church with stained-glass windows and stone arches.

Grandpa turns on the lights and the heat and gets out the broom to sweep the entry. Father Ziegler still stands there, looking around our plain little church with twelve pews to sit on, six clear glass windows, a piano in the back, and a little altar that Dad and Grandpa made out of an oak that came down on the ranch almost thirty years ago.

"It used to be a schoolhouse," I say, walking back down the middle aisle toward the new priest.

"Beautiful." He takes a deep breath. "Did someone build that altar specifically for this church?"

"Well, yeah." I steal a look at Grandpa but I don't say anything, because humility is very big with him.

"It's perfect," Father Ziegler goes on. "Exactly the right size for the room, and the same proportion as the windows."

So now we know he'll get along with Grandpa even if he doesn't get along with anyone else. Not that Grandpa's a parishioner or anything, so the jury is still out as far as I'm concerned.

Grandma and Grandpa finish their tidying up and

meet each other by the church door, just like they have forever. They hold hands and bow their heads until their foreheads touch. They only pray for a few seconds, and then Grandpa kisses Grandma, and she strokes the side of his face. He zips up his coat and goes outside, and she takes up her usual pew.

I secretly love that little minute the Grands spend together before church, because it gives me a solid feeling of we-will-make-it-through-no-matter-what-happens. But now that I see Father Ziegler watching them, I wonder what he's thinking. I bet his grandparents don't have a problem with going to the same church.

So I say, "He likes to sit outside and listen to his Inner Light on a Sunday." Father nods very seriously at this, and then I say, "And he writes his Sunday letters," in case listening to Inner Light sounds just a little too much like something a New Age hippie would do.

"Is he in the Society of Friends?"

I nod, but I'm impressed already. He's a lot quicker on the uptake than your average priest. Most people don't know Friends is the right word for Quakers. We both look out the window to see Grandpa sitting at the picnic table with a thermos of coffee and the morning sun on his back as he sets out letters, a journal, and a pen with the care of a surgeon. It's not fair that there isn't another Quaker for a hundred miles for him to pray with, so he writes to three different Quaker pastors every week, and they write to him.

We hear cars in the gravel lot, so Father and I head to the sacristy to get ready for Mass. Just as I am about to close the sacristy door, Mrs. Hobbs comes in to warm up the piano. I can tell it's her because I think she dips her entire wardrobe in lilac perfume.

My heart sinks a little when I see her, because she has an opera-high voice that is so thin it makes you think of starving stray cats. Before Dad's unit left for Iraq, Paco's dad used to lead the singing. He has a deep, round voice. To be fair, it is the sort of voice that makes you think of beer and polka, but people can sing along to that sort of voice—which, in my opinion, is the whole point of having someone to lead the songs in the first place.

I listen to Mrs. Hobbs play as families shuffle in and find their seats. I take the white altar boy alb out of the closet, pull it on over my clothes, and check the mirror to be sure it hangs evenly all the way to the floor. I stand up a little straighter, like my dad and brothers do when they're in uniform. Half a dozen thick white cords with a knot on each end hang on the back of the closet door. I pick the shortest one and make a belt of it, with the extra rope hanging down on the right side of the robe. Back when I was starting out and Frank was still in eighth grade, he showed me how to do the right kind of knot, and we served together on the altar for the whole summer. Now I do it alone. Paco and I trade off every other Sunday.

Father Ziegler stands at the other closet and puts on an alb and rope like me, but he puts a stole over the top, the purple one for Lent. It's two minutes to nine, so I get out the tall brass candlelighter and slide a half inch of wick out of the holder. Father fishes a lighter out of his pocket, which is weird because he doesn't smell like a smoker. We get the wick lit, and I carry it out to light the altar candles. I take a quick look. Paco and Rosita are sitting in the front row with all their aunts and uncles. Their *abuelo* and *abuela* sit by the window, holding hands, and they have two whole rows of cousins. Ernesto is sitting in the back with the three other shepherds that work in the valley. I think one of those guys is his cousin and the other two are from his home village. They lean their heads together to share the Spanish missal that Ernesto brings with him every Sunday.

"Are they ready?" Father asks when I come back into the sacristy with the candlelighter.

"Yup."

For a second I think he's just going to dash out there and dive into it, but then he leans back on the closet door, closes his eyes, and bows his head. I'm going to like this one, I can tell—not too bossy or fussy, but he looks like the type to pay attention to the important stuff.

Mrs. Hobbs starts the opening hymn, and Father Ziegler and I go to the back of the church. Everyone stands up, and I lead Father up the center aisle, carrying the cross and walking like a soldier. When we get to the front of the church, I put the cross in its holder and Father Ziegler kisses the altar. I bring him the book and hold it up for the opening blessing. I don't know why he needs it. I know all the words by heart already.

I love the rhythm of the Mass, and being there at exactly the right time with the book for Father to read the blessing, or the water for washing, or the chalice and paten in exactly the right place on the altar. The people sit and kneel and stand, and then, at the holiest moment, when Father holds the bread and wine up to heaven, I ring one small bell. There is a hush while that moment echoes off the walls of this place, just like it has for centuries all over the world. No matter what happens to Dad or the ranch, the Mass is always going to be the same.

After the opening blessing, Mrs. Hobbs launches into the Gloria a full two octaves above human range. Somewhere there are dogs getting spiritual edification from this. The rest of us are just bumbling along in search of a key. Fortunately, she trails off and doesn't repeat the chorus. Mary Gail steps up quick for the first reading just in case Mrs. Hobbs decides to launch into another verse.

Mary Gail is Grandma's best friend. I love to listen to her read. She can put out the word of God with real conviction. If any of us are thinking about worshiping Babylonian gods like it says in Exodus, Mary Gail's tone of voice pretty much sets us straight.

Then we are in trouble again with the psalm. Father Ziegler stands up to read it, but he's only three words in when there's a bang from the piano and Mrs. Hobbs starts singing the psalm. It's an easy mistake to make. Some folks sing the psalm and some don't. Father sits back down, and everything goes fine until the Gospel. He gets up and goes to the lectern to read. He waits for us to sing the Alleluia first, but there isn't a note or a squawk from Mrs. Hobbs at the piano. She has her back to us, so Father can't make eye contact to find out if a song is supposed to go there. So finally we just say the Alleluia and the awkward moment passes.

The preaching goes okay, once you get used to the New York accent. Unfortunately, after the preaching we are right back to the problem of when to sing and when not to sing. By the time we come to the final blessing, even the back of Mrs. Hobbs's head looks angry.

"Well, that went all right, except for the music," Father Ziegler says as soon as we walk through the sacristy door at the end of Mass.

"Mrs. Hobbs looked pretty steamed to me," I say, unknotting the rope around my alb.

"I'll talk to her," Father says.

"I'd give her a few days to get over it."

"It doesn't seem right to let bad feelings fester."

I set the book of Scriptures back in the drawer and pull out the parish directory. "E-mail her."

He thinks it over for a minute. "That might work."

I shrug, pull off the alb, and hang it in the closet between the alb I used to wear when I was ten and the one I'll wear when I'm taller.

He takes off his stole and folds it in half. "You

seem to know a lot about the parish. Is there anything else I should know about?"

"Well . . ." I take the communion cup and plate to the sink and run hot water. "You know, a bunch of us are soldiers and veterans." I stop myself before I say, So don't say anything stupid about the war, but then I wonder if he would even get what I mean.

"Me too." Father Ziegler slides the folded stole onto a hanger. He smiles at my look. "Surprise!"

I take a better look at him now and decide he's not as young as I thought. I rinse out the chalice and dry it.

"What branch?"

"Army—artillery."

"Wow."

"It was loud."

He looks around the sacristy, and I wonder if he thinks washing the chalice and communion plate is his job, because some priests are funny about that. Maybe he's wondering if he can just leave the rest of the after-Mass jobs to me and go to the parish hall to have coffee and grown-up chat. I've never heard of a priest who didn't need a cup of coffee after Mass. This one starts looking through the cupboards. When he gets to the closet, he takes out the broom and starts to sweep, which I've never seen a priest do in my entire life.

"Gee, thanks, Father." I'm about to tell him, You don't really have to do that, when he says, "No problem, glad to help. Thank you . . ." And then he pauses and I wonder if he thinks Brother is a dumb nickname.

"It's okay, really. Everyone calls me Brother."

"Sorry. It's just that the people I call Brother are all really old Jesuits. What's your given name?"

"Ignatius," I mumble into the sink.

"That's a great name," he says, and not like he's making fun of me, either. "Saint Ignatius is the patron saint of every Jesuit priest in the world."

"Yeah, but he's been dead for hundreds of years, hasn't he?"

"Good point. Probably not a great name to have in grade school, is it?"

"No," I say in a huffier voice than I really mean to use. "Paco's dad used to call me Nacho when I was little, but I had to put a stop to that on account of—"

"The cheese?" Father Ziegler smiles. "That's tough. I got in a few fistfights over nicknames in grade school myself."

"Really?"

It's hard to imagine him hitting anyone, but then it's hard to imagine him firing off artillery shells, which must be why they have that saying about books and their covers.

"Yeah." He goes back to the closet for the dustpan. "My mother named me Cornelius John."

"No way!" I finish up with the plate and put the altar pieces in the safe, imagining the sorts of nicknames you could make out of Cornelius. All the ones I can think of are pretty insulting.

"You think I would make that up?"

"So what do your friends call you?"

"CJ."

"CJ? Really?"

"Yeah."

"That's a girl name."

"You got a problem with that, punk?" he says, and bangs the dustpan empty against the side of the garbage can. " 'Cause if you do, you can just step outside and we'll settle it."

For a minute there I think, Boy, the bishop really sent us a wacky one this time, but then I see he's kidding, so I laugh and say, "Okay, truce."

"I've got a better idea," he says. "You think of a cooler nickname for me and I'll think of one for you. Deal?"

"Deal."

And then we go back into the church, because it's empty now. All the people are in the parish hall with the coffee cake and doughnuts. He takes the candles off the altar, and I fold up the purple altar cloth.

Usually, when I'm doing the after-Mass work, I'm thinking about the week ahead and wondering if Dad even gets to go to Mass. Probably not, because they only get a chaplain once a month, and he's a Baptist. So it's actually a nice change to be thinking of a name for Cornelius that isn't totally stupid. But when I get to the last job I start dawdling, because it's hard to think of one. Just when I think I can't go another minute without a frosted maple bar, I say "Conn," and show Father Ziegler the cabinet where we hide the keys.

"Con?" He frowns a little and starts locking up the cupboards.

"Yeah, like Take the Conn, Lieutenant, and fire the torpedoes."

"Oh, *Hunt for Red October*." He smiles. "Good book. Conn. I could get used to that."

"Plus, it has a hint of artillery in it, and I think it's always a good idea to sound a little bit dangerous."

He laughs and opens the back door of the sacristy, which goes to the parking lot.

"How about Natch for you?"

I try it on in my mind a couple times, and then I imagine how the boys at school would say it. But it sounds okay to me, and he was a good sport about the name I picked, so I say, "Yeah, perfect."

We walk across the lot to the parish hall and he says, "Hey, Natch," and then he nods back in the direction of the church. "You have a talent for that sort of thing, you know. Thanks."

PROMISES MADE

APRIL

"Color guard, advance," our teacher says, and the two third graders bring the flag to the pole. It's their first time, so they are super serious. They unfold it slowly and clip it to the line. The rest of us, twenty-three in all, stand in a ring around the flagpole, lined up from little Colleen in kindergarten to Bud, three times her size, in eighth grade. I love flag ceremony in spring because there are still flowers on the weeds, and the wind isn't hot and dry yet. The color guard runs the flag all the way up and then lowers it to half-staff because a soldier from Oregon died three days ago. He's not someone from Dad's unit; still, I hate to see the flag snapping in the wind in the middle of the pole. We say the pledge and then have a moment of silence. I close my eyes and whisper the names of the soldiers from our school that went to Iraq: four dads and a mom in the primary room, three in the upper-grade room. I say a double blessing for Paco and Rosita, because their folks are both in Dad's battalion.

We crowd up the schoolhouse steps. The little kids turn right into the primary room and the big kids turn left. On the way to class, Paco says, "Hey, Brother," and he gives the secret sign, like he has every morning for the last eight months and twelve days, to say that there wasn't a visit from the rear detachment sergeant who makes the casualty calls to families. I give Rosita a little slug on the shoulder to say I've been praying for her folks.

But when we walk through the classroom door, it's all over, because there is a line down the middle of the room, and everyone has chosen a side. Naturally the girls all sit on one side of the room, the side with the computer lab. They look out on Highway 20, which goes from Boise to Burns. The boys sit on the piano side and look out on a thousand acres of government land. Actually, us boys don't look out the window. We survey the enemy. There are four of them and six of us, unless they form an alliance with the little girls over in the primary room. And then we're in deep trouble, because a seven-year-old girl will follow her captain's orders and a seven-year-old boy just won't, so there isn't much point in diplomacy, near as I can tell.

Here's how the enemy forces are arrayed. Shannon Egan is the ranking seventh grader. She is approximately twelve feet tall and will kick us to death if we don't maintain our perimeter.

Anita Hollowell ought to be second in command because she's the other seventh grader, but she reads constantly, picks her nose, and harbors dead apple cores in her desk. Our best intelligence suggests she is developing their chemical weapons program. This is confirmed by the fact that none of the other girls sit by her at lunch.

Shelby Haskle is second in command on account of her formidable artillery skills. She is an evil genius in devising tank traps and roping adversaries. She's the other half of the Haskle family's junior calf-roping team. Chuck Haskle, her roping partner, is probably a double agent. We send him over to the girls' lunch table to collect intelligence, but he actually enjoys chatting.

Then there is the secret fifth-grade weapon, Rosita Ugarte. She is so little, she is practically invisible, which makes her the perfect spy. There she sits, in the corner, quiet as church, but if you're not careful she'll drop off radar completely, and before you know it your coat sleeves are stapled together. She looks completely innocent, with brown eyes and one long black braid, just like all the other Basque women in her family. She wears a red ribbon at the end of her braid, always red except once in a while it's a white ribbon, obviously a secret signal to attack. When Rosita wears a white ribbon, the boys shift to DEFCON 1 immediately.

You would think, being outnumbered and all, the girls would lose every battle, especially since girls just don't have the attention span for warfare. They keep veering off into piracy or unicorns and griffins, or they all go and morph into princesses, completely against the uniform code. Still, they're much more treacherous than they look, and they can run like wild horses, so according to my count, our battles are dead even, with only a month of school left to break the tie.

Ammunition is always an issue. There are a couple of scrubby pines along the schoolyard fence that drop cones in the fall. With careful hoarding, we can make them last until there are snowballs to throw. Spring is the real problem. We have to wait until April—May sometimes—for the camellias to fall off the bush. On the sheltered side of the school, near where the hose leaks, there is a giant camellia. It's thirty feet tall, with round red flowers every spring. It's kind of dippy to fight with flowers, and sometimes the girls get completely the wrong idea about flower petals and weddings. But I like the way the schoolyard looks like a blood-spattered battlefield after it's covered with red flowers.

Paco and I are the first out the door for morning recess. The little boys come screaming out right after us and take up a defensible position on the jungle gym. The little girls commandeer the swing set.

"Come on, Brother, the armory!" Paco calls over his shoulder. We make it to the camellia bush first and stuff flowers into our sweatshirt hoods, which make the perfect quivers. I see Paco sneaking some flowers that aren't dead yet.

"Just the ones on the ground," I warn him, "or the brass will have our butts in the stockade."

We've almost got them all when Amazon Shannon stomps her foot down in front of the last dozen dropped flowers.

"Don't even think about it!" she snaps. We beat it right away, because that girl can kick like a mule.

We have plenty of firepower, so we retreat to the backstop to plan our strategy. The older boys are heavy artillery all the way. They have been working out some kind of catapult for tumbleweeds for weeks. Paco and me, we love to run, so we cover the light infantry. We're in position for our first charge when that rebel Rosita whips behind me at top speed and snatches a fistful of flowers out of my hood. She must have used some stealth technology. She's pretty much a one-woman aviation brigade.

"Oh man!" Paco groans.

Rosita just turns around and sticks her tongue out at me, and the little girls cheer. She runs back to girl headquarters, where they are maintaining the cover of an innocent game of four square. It would definitely be standard operating procedure to eliminate enemy air cover right off, but Rosie is Paco's little sister, so I hate to press that point.

We get in three good charges and nail Anita for sure, but she doesn't die. She always refuses to die, which is just more proof in my book that she's secretly radioactive. And then Shannon and Shelby corner Paco and pelt him to death with flowers.

I love it when Paco dies. He's read a ton of good

books, so he knows just how to pull it off. Today, he spins around four times and moans, makes a few dizzy staggers, and then collapses in a twitching heap. At last his body goes all quiet and he gets ready to make his death speech. It's always a great speech about some secret conspiracy or hidden explosives. This time it's the location of the treasure, and he dies completely just a second before he can say the one thing that will solve the mystery of where to find the Blood Diamonds.

It's beautiful. I feel noble just kneeling beside him, holding his sleeve. The flower petals that killed him are splashed on the dirt under his head like a halo in the holy pictures.

I should do something for him. There's a hush over the schoolyard, because even the little kids like to watch Paco die. I can hear the flag flap against the pole. Perfect.

I lower the flag and unclip it. I carry it, very formal, over my arm, the way I carry the altar cloth when I serve at Mass. I drape it over Paco's body. The little kids are stone-still, their mouths hanging open with reverence, except for Rosita. She's got a little wobble in her chin. After my speech, I'll fold the flag in a triangle and give it to her. It's only proper for the surviving sister to get it. I'm about to say my piece when Rosita rockets behind me and sweep-kicks me behind the knees. I fall like a tree.

"He's my brother. You can't have him!"

She snatches the flag off his body like it's laundry and stomps over to the flagpole. Her shoulders are shaking with rage, and she runs that flag all the way to the top.

A truck pulls up alongside the schoolyard fence. Three men get out. They are wearing clean boots, white shirts, and black hats: Paco and Rosita's uncles. The second I see them, all the breath squeezes out of my chest. They would never leave the ranch together in the middle of the working day, not in their Sunday clothes. I look down at Paco and hold out my hand.

He grabs hold to stand up, and for a minute I want to take him and run away and live off the land like bandits so he won't ever have to face that bad-news row of uncles.

But then Rosita sees them, and what can I do? I can't let her hear what happened alone. My mouth is suddenly too dry to say anything. I nod my head in the direction of the fence. Paco turns and looks. He goes straight to the flagpole, where Rosita stands wide-eyed and frozen. The little kids keep on swinging and running, but the big kids get what's going on. They stop and stare. Pretty soon the whole playground gets spooky-quiet.

Paco and Rosita head over to the gate, and I follow some respectful paces behind. When they get there, I see Paco make himself stand like a soldier, and I lift up my head and put my shoulders back, but I still feel just as hollow and shaky inside.

The oldest uncle takes Rosita's two hands in his and kneels in front of her.

"They're alive, *mi niña*. They are both alive and coming home."

Rosita starts to cry because there is only one reason to send a soldier home early. Her uncle holds her and rocks her while she cries, and the other two turn to Paco.

"They're hurt, but they're going to live. The army will fly them to a hospital in Germany in the morning."

"We spoke to Colonel Alderman just now. He promises they will recover."

I hear Paco pulling in big gulps of air and trying not to cry. My whole body feels hot with shame because my dad's okay and his isn't. I want to hug him, but his *tíos* are already there, with their broad arms over his shoulders. They make a circle of grief that closes me out.

A second car pulls up, with all the aunts inside. Paco's *abuela* gets out and goes to the schoolhouse steps to talk to our teacher. The oldest uncle says, "Come with us now. We'll go to church tonight at the cathedral in Boise, and then in the morning Abuela will go to be with them at the hospital in Frankfurt."

Rosita just looks at the ground, and Paco nudges her toward the cars. I should say something. I take a step closer.

"Mr. Ugarte, may I come help with the stock at your place?"

They all turn and look at me.

"Grandpa and I could drive over after school and make sure everything is squared away for the night."

"*Gracias,*" the oldest uncle says without smiling. "Our doors are open. You will see what to do."

"I'll take care of everything."

They get in their cars and drive off. Already I feel that promise on my shoulders, and I'm calculating how to get my chores done faster to have enough time. Grandpa will come help because it's in his code of how to treat people, and Ernesto never complains about extra work. Still, I'm the one who promised.

I think about my dad loading the Ugartes on a plane for Germany, and promising to call their brothers, and promising he would check up on them to make sure they get treated right.

I could never do it. I couldn't make all those promises. I could never take those salutes and the "yes, sirs" and then take moms and dads into danger. God knows what I'm supposed to be—not a soldier.

BOOTS ON THE GROUND

MAY

"*Bueno,* Ignacio. Can you feel the calf?" Ernesto says. He is standing with me in the birthing stall, holding the cow's head so she won't back up and step on me. I've helped with calving since I was eight, but Dad never let me pull a calf before, and now I know why. Last year my arm was too short.

"Lean into it, Brother," Grandpa says. He puts a hand on my shoulder and shows me how to turn a little sideways and get a few inches further into the birth canal so I can reach the baby calf. Grandpa pulled the last two calves, and now he's leaning on the bars of the stall to rest. The cow bawls pitifully. She's a first-calf heifer, and she doesn't know what she's doing. Ernesto brought her inside when her labor went on too long.

"Don't worry, she's just scared. You aren't hurting her," Grandpa says.

I grunt and nod, standing in the wet, sticky straw. Grandma's in the stall next to us, making sure the calves we just pulled can stand and drink. There are five more calves with the mothers who didn't need any help at the far end of the barn. The sour, salty smell of blood and goo makes me gag a little, so I breathe through my mouth.

"*Muy bien.* Find the feet—two feet—and pull," Ernesto says.

I grope around, twisting my wrist from side to side. At first all I feel is wet fur, and then something roundish and bumpy—a nose, maybe. I work my way down. At last! A leg! It's broomstick-skinny. I fish around for the other one and squeeze them tight in my fist.

"I found them!"

"*Bravo.* Now pull, Ignacio."

"Nice and steady, Brother; the hardest part is done." Grandpa holds the tail to one side so I don't get smacked in the head with it.

I take a deep breath and pull as steady as I can. I feel the calf's legs and head ease out of the womb and into the birth canal.

"Here she comes," I grunt, leaning back.

I brace myself for another tug, but something sucks the calf backward and pulls me in with it.

"No! Wait! Hey, she's going backwards."

"*Sí,*" Ernesto says. "It is like the waves of the ocean. Pull with the wave, not against."

This doesn't seem like a good time to point out that I've never been to the beach in my whole life.

"He's right, Brother, don't fight the contraction. Pull when you feel the squeeze and hold when it lets up. Do you feel it?"

I've been trying not to think about my arm getting squeezed every other minute, because, honestly, it's a really gross feeling.

"*Sí,* like the ocean." Ernesto presses my free hand on the heifer's belly so I can feel the wave from the inside and the outside. "Pull. Wait. Pull. Wait."

"Great. Thanks." I push that queasy feeling out of my mind and think about what I guess the ocean is like. I brace my free arm on the heifer's hipbone and pull and wait and pull.

"It feels . . . like my arm . . . is going to fall off."

Ernesto smiles. "No, you are gaining. *¡Fantástico!*"

I lean back and pull some more. Every inch of me that isn't inside the heifer is drenched with sweat. My hand gets a cramp, and my grip slips down to the hooves. Every muscle in my arm and back and shoulders feels like it's going to snap.

"How does Dad . . . manage to pull . . . a dozen calves a day?"

"He has you to help," Grandpa says, "and Grandma and your brothers. Nobody is strong enough to do this alone."

"I don't think . . . I'm strong enough . . . to do this even once." But just as I say it, the calf finally slips all the way out of the womb and into the birth canal, and suddenly I'm only in up to my elbow.

"*Muy bien,* almost there." Ernesto gives the cow a pat on the shoulder. "*Tranquila, mi vaca. No temas.*"

"Hey! It isn't so hard now. Here it comes!" I tug the last few inches and two little hooves poke out. Another tug and I see a nose. Suddenly the heifer figures out what she should do, and the calf squirts out so fast I fall over backward and thump! eighty pounds of wet, bloody calf lands on my chest.

"Well, look at you," Grandma says, glancing over the top of the stall next door.

I'd rather not. I'm sure I've never looked more revolting.

"We'll make a rancher out of this boy yet," she says.

Grandpa reaches out a hand to help me stand up. "This boy might have his own road to follow."

"Do you think?" Grandma says, looking me over more carefully.

"Time will show," Grandpa says.

Grandma reaches out and messes up my hair. "Don't you let that road take you too far from us."

Even though every muscle in my body aches, I can't stop smiling. Dad will be so proud of me when I tell him. The calf shivers and blinks open her eyes. I rub the goo off her face. The heifer turns around and starts licking her calf clean with earnest concentration. I hold the calf just long enough to know she's breathing steadily and then slide her onto the cleanest patch of straw I can find in the pen. Ernesto tosses me a rag to wipe off the slime. The blood doesn't seem nearly so gross to me, now that I'm really helping with the birth. It just feels like a natural part of the work, as clean and honest as dirt on the ground or sweat on a horse.

I kneel beside my calf and stroke her fur. She's going to be a beautiful rusty red when she dries off, just like her mom. She has huge brown eyes and the saddest little face. I hold out my hand to her, and she immediately tries to suck on my fingers.

"She's a fine strong one," Grandma says, and then she turns to Grandpa. "Look at that boy shaking. When is the last time we fed this child?"

I shrug and try to hold my arms still. "I dunno. Lunch?"

"For heaven's sake, that was seven hours ago. There's a pot of stew on the stove. You eat; we'll finish up here and catch up with you."

I nod and slide open the barn door. The long evening shadow of the cottonwood tree reaches all the way from the barn to the front steps. I stop by the hose at the side of the house to wash the rest of the goop off my hands and arms. I kick off my boots, slide out of my work clothes, and run into the house in my shorts.

All the lights are out, and the house is weirdly quiet. I triple-wash my hands in the sink, click on the evening news, and dish up a big bowl of stew. I take it to the sofa in the living room.

There's a roadside bomb on the news. Again. It seems like there's one every night. The TV flashes pictures of burning trucks and gaping holes in the pavement and people wandering around, dazed and weary. Every time I see it I want to turn it off, but I stay and search the edges of the picture for Dad. But he's never there, and they never say the names of the dead.

I used to like the news when Dad was home. We would put it on every evening after chores, and Dad and I would find the news stories in the atlas. If the big brothers were home, they would make pretend bets on the sports, and everyone watched the weather.

Grandpa has kept track of the local weather every day for the last forty-eight years. He keeps a log in his journal of the daily temperature at six o'clock in the morning, noon, and nine o'clock at night, along with the barometer reading, wind direction, and rainfall. Sometimes I watch him copy it out in tidy block print in the plain black journal he writes in every evening after supper. He always looks up from his writing for the weather, checking the local report for accuracy and keeping an eye on communities in Montana, Nebraska, and Washington where he has friends.

Sometimes I see him sigh and shake his head at the weathermen, especially the young ones. "They don't account for the shape of the land," he would grumble. If it looked like anyone was paying attention, he'd launch into his personal philosophy of the weather.

"The land makes weather as much as the sky," he would say, demonstrating the contours of a landscape with his hand. "The shape of the hills and the amount of water in the ground." And then he'd lean back in the La-Z-Boy and say, "Land shapes a man's heart, too, and his aspirations. A man near the mountains learns to look up, and it calls his mind to God." And then he'd do that Quaker thing where he sits quietly and says nothing, and the rest of us go back to playing chess or poker, and a dozen hands later he would say something like, "God's in the valleys, too, in the coolness of the water and the softness of the ground. That's the tender side of the Almighty."

I love it when he talks like that, because then, when I go wading in the creek, I think of the Holy Spirit squooshing up between my toes.

Now I turn off the news and get the atlas from the bookshelf in Dad's room. I sit on the edge of his bed and flip it open to the Middle East. Nothing but flat land in the entire nation of Iraq. Well, okay, maybe a few hills around the edge. For real mountains you have to go east to Iran or north to Turkey. What's Dad going to look at on all that level ground? It's not even nice tidy deserts like in Saudi Arabia. Iraq's got swamps, and every picture I ever see on the news just looks dirty and depressing. What's going to lift him up over there?

Cities are even worse. Dad can barely stand Boise. I don't know how he's coping with Baghdad. Whenever we have to go to town for something, Dad maps out the route and timetable like it's a mission. He gets us in and out of there in two hours tops.

I asked him about it once and he said, "In the city, they never look at you when you walk by. To get a friendly smile or a civil greeting, you have to buy something."

I hear Grandma and Grandpa and Ernesto on the front porch, talking about tomorrow's work. I head back to the kitchen, put on a pot of coffee for them, and grab a handful of cookies for me. I sit down at Grandma's computer and log on to the chat room the brothers have on Sunday nights.

FRANKenstein: Hey, Brother, what's the news? How are the Grands?

I wipe the cookie crumbs off my fingers and type in an answer.

IGuanodon: It's calving this week. The Grands are tired but fine.

PyroPETE: Hola amigos, what's the news? I'm the staff duty officer tonight for the battalion. It's hotter than habaneros down here.

IGuanodon: I pulled a calf just now. It was great! How are your soldiers? Did you blow anything up today?

PyroPETE: Nope, land mines were last week.

JOHNBronco: Good job on the calf, Brother. Your arms are going to be killing you tomorrow.

PyroPETE: Didn't you and Jim have a college rodeo this week?

JOHNBronco: We medaled in team roping. I took third in bronc riding, but Jim tanked. Dead last. Bad horse. He made up for it at the dance afterward. Now he's got a bunch of city chicks on his MySpace. Like that's going to work out.

Jim is a better dancer than all of the rest of us put together. For one thing, he can remember both steps of the two-step. Plus, he's brave enough to ask a girl to dance. I'm never going to do that. Not in a million years.

IGuanodon: Hey guys, we should talk about branding.

JOHNBronco: What's to talk about?

IGuanodon: I think we should go with acid branding this

year. It's easier, cheaper, and not so hard on the calves. I'm just saying because some of the calves will be yours.

FRANKenstein: Still afraid of that hot iron? Get over it. You're not a little kid anymore.

JOHNBronco: You should have a branding party, Brother. You never have any fun. How are you going to get a girlfriend if you don't get a chance to impress the ladies with your roping and tying?

As if!

PyroPETE: Dad likes the hot brand better. I think we should stick to his way. He's counting on us to get it right while he's gone.

IGuanodon: Dad always had 5 sons and a dozen neighbors. I've got nothing!!!

I shouldn't have said that. That was a stupid thing to say.

IGuanodon: There just aren't enough men around here to do a regular branding. Are you guys going to be home in June?

PyroPETE: Sorry, Brother, come summer we've got orders to train up soldiers heading to Iraq. Nine months straight. All leaves canceled.

Oh man, if Pete doesn't come it just won't work, because Jim and John will fight over who's in charge and Frank will spend the whole time assigning the icky jobs to me.

IGuanodon: The army's supposed to give you 30 days leave a year. What happened?

PyroPETE: I wish I could be there, but a training mission is still a mission. Sorry.

FRANKenstein: Buck up, Brother. We don't need Pete to babysit us. John, when are you and Jim home for the summer?

JOHNBronco: Hate to tell you this, but Jim and I have Cadet Advanced Course up at Fort Lewis for a month in June. Same deal. No way to weasel out.

IGuanodon: Wait, who's going to take the cattle up to the mountains?

JOHNBronco: We'll be back in time for cow camp. It'll make for longer days with just me, Jim, and Frank up there, but we'll manage.

FRANKenstein: I'll be there, Brother. I'll be done with school in three weeks.

This is the other half of Frank's extreme bossiness—extreme loyalty, which is why I don't hate his guts. Trouble is, it doesn't solve the problem. There's no way

you can round up, rope, brand, and castrate every calf
who needs it with one teenager and one kid, even with
Grandpa and the hired man helping out.

PyroPETE: You've got good neighbors out there. When I
was your age, we went to a half dozen branding parties a year.
Those folks will help us now.

He just doesn't get it. Nothing is the same with
Dad gone. Pete hasn't lived at home since he went
away to board at the high school.

IGuanodon: Mr. Haskle's been pulling double shifts at the
gas station so Arnie won't have to close it down while he's in Iraq.
Mr. Egan's got back trouble, and he's already taken on the Jasper
ranch next door. You can't ask people for favors they aren't able to
give you.

There's a long pause, and I know my brothers are
kicking table legs and muttering swears, but I don't
care. They aren't in combat. It's their job to worry.
They're not the ones who have to look at the Grands
after they've worked for ten hours straight and the
gate's still not fixed and the wood's not split or stacked

and the tractor engine is still in eight pieces on the back porch. I'd ditch school myself and do it, except Grandma would murder me on the spot.

PyroPETE: That's enough. Brother is the one boots on the ground at home. This branding decision is entirely his call.

IGuanodon: Thanks, Pete. Don't worry about it, guys. We'll do a good job. Grandpa and I are a pretty good team.

I put the computer on standby, drop my dishes in the sink, and head outside. It's almost dark, and the ground still holds some heat from the day. I stop at my tire swing and sit. The air is cool on my bare arms, and frogs are singing love songs down by the water. There are a few clucks and flaps from the hens settling into the chicken shed for the night, and Ike gets in the last word with the rest of the horses just so they all remember who's the boss horse in the morning. Sheep have got nothing to say at night on account of there are things out there that eat them. But our sheepdog, Donner, has started his night patrol around the edge of the flock, sniffing the wind and watching the shadows.

I think about Dad standing upside down to me on the other side of the world, with the sun just coming up. He's got a cup of coffee and a desk stacked a dozen deep in maps. His driver, Arnie, is there, and the company captains, planning the day's business. I bet my dad turns away from them for a minute to take in the sky and picture me sitting here, taking good care of his land. I love knowing that we are imagining the same thing at the same time, and I send him the hug of knowing his home is here, right here, safe and green no matter how hot the wind blows where he has gone.

THE VETERANS

JUNE

The thing I love about having Frank home from school is that I can beat him at chess at least half the time. The thing I don't love is that he drives. He just got his permit and now he needs a hundred hours behind the wheel, so Grandma is letting him drive us down to the VFW hall in the next town over. She chats away with him while he's driving, like this is perfectly safe. Grandpa actually falls asleep. Obviously these two have never played Matchbox cars with Frank; otherwise they'd know how much he loves to crash into things. I keep a close eye on the traffic and the speedometer from the backseat. I'm exhausted by the time we've gone twenty miles. At least when he goes up to cow camp in a few weeks, he'll be off the road.

The social event of the season around here is the Memorial Day dinner down at the local VFW. They changed it to June this year to make it a welcome home party, because Mr. and Mrs. Ugarte are back from Iraq. We aren't going to see the rest of them for ages because Dad's unit got extended until the end of November.

I wish I could say the Ugartes are back safe and sound, but Paco and Rosita's dad left a fair piece of himself behind. He's been at the army hospital in Washington, D.C., getting fitted for a leg, and Mrs. Ugarte was treated for burn injuries right alongside him.

They got back to town a week ago. Paco and Rosita took the whole week off from school to be with them. Tonight's the first time I'll see them as a real family again.

Bald truth is, I felt a lot better about the Ugartes being home before I found out that Dad's tour in Iraq will be extended. It's stupid. I know it's stupid. It's probably even a sin, but ever since I heard a week ago, I've been thinking, It's not fair. They've got somebody home with them. Every other kid in the battalion's got one civilian parent. It's just me who's doing this alone.

But now that I see the local veterans rolling in,

with the shoulder-slapping and the way they look at each other, like they're better than brothers, it's not so bad. It loosens me up to hear the rumble of their talk.

The hall's nearly full when Mr. and Mrs. Ugarte step into the room. Conversations drop off, and one after another, the veterans stand up and clap. There isn't any shouting or cheering. I don't even see smiles. In fact, it's the saddest applause I've ever heard in my life. And then, one by one, with plenty of space in between, the old vets come up and shake Mr. and Mrs. Ugarte's hand and say, "Welcome home, soldier."

I head to the chow line to help serve up. Rosita is already in the kitchen, in a pink summer dress, hustling plates back and forth. I'm ready to give her the "good to see you again" slug on the shoulder or maybe flick a chunk of potato at her, but she's deep in the flock of her aunties, and it wouldn't be worth my life to do her a kindness now. I stand beside Grandpa, who is cutting up pies, and serve warm squares of corn bread.

Most of the veterans are already in line for the chow, and the little kids are cutting in. Father Ziegler is standing off to the side of the room with Mrs. Ugarte, his head leaning close to listen to her. Mr. Ugarte is getting ready to sit down when he unbuckles something from his belt and his whole leg drops out of his pants and clunks on the floor.

I feel that clunk deep in the pit of my stomach. Knowing someone has lost a leg is not nearly the same as seeing a fake leg come off of a real person's body.

Mr. Ugarte slides his leg onto the table, slaps a stirrup down beside it, and sits down. In minutes, he's hard at it with Nathan, the saddlemaker out of Pendleton, and McTigue, the bronzesmith from Wallowa Lake. I hear "fitting" and "torque" and "safety release" in their talk, and they fiddle with the wires and rods on the leg like it's some wayward tractor part. Grandma is in the thick of that conversation, sketching out ideas on a paper napkin. They must be figuring out how to get Mr. Ugarte up on a horse.

I keep scooping up pieces of corn bread and plopping them on plates, but I can't stop looking at Mr. Ugarte's empty pants leg dangling under the table. I know whose fault it is that he's crippled. My dad gave those orders. He looked at that map and approved the route and assigned the driver. I see that swinging pants leg shaking a finger at me: Your fault, your fault, your fault.

What does Paco think? I didn't see him come in

with Rosita, and he hasn't come through the food line, either. It's not like him to hold back on eating. The last time I saw him was the day he left school early to get his folks from the airport. That last recess he pushed me down, said a Basque swear, and kicked me. Then he just walked away. I don't even know what to say about that. We've been friends since before kindergarten and we fight all the time, but kicking and cussing aren't the same as fighting. Maybe he just didn't want to come tonight. Can't say I blame him. I don't think I could force food down at gunpoint now.

I slide away from the serving table and head out the back door. I sit down on the steps and stare at the gravel parking lot, which isn't much of a view. But then I see Paco's mom.

She's smoking. Paco's mom does not smoke.

She's pacing at the edge of the parking lot and talking to herself. She has her sleeve pulled all the way down to her fingers to cover up the bumpy part of her burn scar, and I can see that her arm doesn't go all the way straight.

I wonder if my dad smokes. I try to picture him lighting a cigarette with his hand cupped around the match like in the old cowboy movies. It doesn't fit the dad I remember from eleven months ago. He always had something else in his hands—the reins, or the steering wheel, or a tool and something that needed fixing. In the morning it was coffee in the blue mug, and at night the newspaper or a book.

I don't even know what he does all day now. His e-mails are full of nothing—a sandstorm one day, kids playing street soccer the next. What if he comes back different and I don't recognize him? What if he doesn't know me and . . . I turn those thoughts right around, because it's bad luck to think scary things.

I lean my elbows back on the step behind me and take in the sky. It's only just getting dark, but maybe I'll stay and look for my stars. I almost don't hear Mrs. Ugarte walk up.

"Hey, Brother," she says. She snuffs out her cigarette on the bottom step, examines the remaining two inches, and puts it in her shirt pocket. I don't know what to say to her, so I smile and try to ignore the cigarette smell.

"Can I sit?" she says. I nod and she looks under the stairs and up at the roof and down the road. I scoot to one side of the step and she joins me. I want to ask about how my dad is—not the news, but what is really happening to him. I'm trying to think how to start when she says, "It's pretty here."

I just nod, because there's nothing to see but a gravel parking lot and empty level sagebrush. You can't even see the mountains.

"It smells good too."

"I like to watch bats sometimes," I say, and I point to the live oak at the edge of the parking lot. The bats have woken up in the last few minutes, and now they are swooping out of the branches and tumbling and twirling around the parking lot light. "They must be so strong to fly like that, but they're tiny."

"They never crash into each other," Mrs. Ugarte says, "even when there are hundreds of them. That's pretty great."

"Were there bats in Iraq?"

Mrs. Ugarte shakes her head. "I never saw one, but maybe they live out in the country. Most of the places we drove to were close to Baghdad." She reaches into her pocket and takes out the cigarette. She rolls it in her fingers for a minute and puts it away. "Where we stayed, there were bright lights all night long and the sound of engines and the smell of diesel." She wrinkles her nose at the memory of it.

I remember that smell on Dad's uniform when he used to come home from field exercises.

"I love that smell," I say. "But I guess I'd get tired of it if there was nothing else."

"You remind me of your mother," Mrs. Ugarte says. "She was easy to talk to. I miss her."

I only have little-kid memories of Mom.

"You are like her, you know. She saw beauty in things other people missed. She didn't just make art, she looked for it, you know? She made it part of her life."

I turn and look at her. "I can't draw or paint like Mom. I can barely color in the lines."

Mrs. Ugarte takes out the cigarette again and lights it. She takes a long pull and blows a smoke ring.

"Whoa, how did you do that?" I say, and then right away I regret approving of smoking.

She says a word that I'm pretty sure is a Basque swear, on account of I hear it all the time at branding when someone drops one of the hot irons or when some calf kicks a person in the head. Not that I've heard a direct translation or anything.

"The thing about war," she says, "is that most of the time it's just brain-killing boredom. The terrifying parts only last a few seconds. Smoking is what they invented to fill up the boring parts."

I have to smile, because this is what I've always liked about Mrs. Ugarte. She has a reason for things, and she's not afraid to tell you about them. On my first day of first grade, when she brought Rosita to kindergarten, she said, "Don't you slug my Rosie, now, because she's going to slug you straight back."

I tested it out anyway. She was telling the truth. You can count on her for that.

"Your mother wasn't much of a gal for coloring inside the lines either, as I recall. I don't claim to know all of your mom's business, but I'm dead sure she'd tell you not to worry about the lines. 'Make your own lines, son.' That's what she would say."

I don't really like to talk about my mom, since she up and moved to New York to sell her paintings when I was five. And then she moved all the way to Rome. That's practically Babylon, to hear folks in town tell it.

Mrs. Ugarte puts her hand on my sleeve, but only for a second. "She's good at being an artist, like your dad's good at being a commanding officer. When you have a gift like that, it kills your soul not to use it."

"He's good at being a rancher. He's good at being my dad. Why isn't it enough for him to stay home and be my dad?"

Mrs. Ugarte leans forward, resting her elbows on

her knees. The smoke from her cigarette rises in a thin curl. I can see her burn scar up close. It looks like dragon skin.

"Don't confuse the right thing with the easy thing, Brother. Sometimes choosing what's right for you breaks your heart." She crushes out her cigarette on the step. Her hand retreats back up her sleeve and she gives a little shrug. "A person can live a little bit broken," she says. "Most of us do, I guess."

I throw bits of gravel from the step back into the parking lot. I can't say as I know what's right for me. Being Paco's friend is all I can think of. Maybe he needs to punch me a few more times before we are friends again. I guess I won't die of it. I hop up and head inside to look for him. If Paco is here, he'll be in the kitchen with the rest of the guys on KP. I grab a stack of dirty plates and head in there.

Paco's already got the cool job of blasting the goop off the plates with the sink hose, so I take the sweaty job of pulling steamy dishes out of the washer and stacking them in the cupboards. It's too noisy to talk, so we work side by side while the long-haired Nam vets with the scary tattoos wash pots. Frank and some of the other high school kids wipe tables and clear the hall. Once the dishes are put away, I break out the last of the home-brewed root beer I've been hiding in Grandpa's cooler. I get one for Paco and we lean on the kitchen counter, looking out into the dining hall.

"Look, Paco," I say, staring down at the hand-drawn root beer label. "I'm sorry about your dad's leg. I'm really sorry. My dad should have checked the map better, or chosen a different route, or gone himself."

I'm searching for other should-haves when Paco cuts me off by setting up our bottles to be goalposts and shooting the root beer cap through.

"S'okay," Paco says, concentrating on his shot. "Now I know how it's all going to come out." He flicks the cap and it slides through the goal, ringing against a bottle as it passes.

"You know how you wonder, What if they die or what if they get captured or what if they just never come home?"

He slides me the cap so I can take a few shots, and I'm glad I don't have to answer, because I know exactly what he's talking about.

"Well, now I know," Paco goes on. "Dad turned into a gimp with a hot temper, and Mom turned into a person who smokes. It's not great, but the bad things I imagined happening to them—they were a lot worse."

I focus on shooting the cap between the root beer bottles.

"So Grandpa says we're butchering a pig next week. You want to come over and help?"

Paco waits until I've taken a sip from my root beer and says, "Is that a seventh-grade pig or an eighth-grade pig?"

I laugh so hard, brown foam comes gushing out my nose.

Fortunately, the grown-ups are too busy tuning up instruments to bug us about foaming boogers. Old Benz has a fiddle, Father Ziegler sets up a washtub bass, Mr. Ugarte unpacks his accordion, and McTigue has one of those Irish drums with the short double-ended drumstick. Mr. Ugarte squeezes out a few measures of something kind of familiar and calls out, "Rosita, Paco, dance for me."

Paco groans, but only loud enough for me to hear.

"Don't worry," I whisper. "I won't tell a soul at school. Promise."

Paco takes Rosita's hand and they do a silly bow and curtsy to each other, and then I see Rosita make him wait and count out a measure so they start on the right step. I don't remember what the dance is called, but it's got a lot of hops in it, and Paco gets to swing Rosita in a circle really fast. Pretty soon people are clapping, and the aunties are singing along, and Paco gets Rosita laughing, and Mr. Ugarte is playing with gusto while big tears roll down his face. Paco and Rosita go faster and faster, but they've still got all the steps perfect. If he weren't my best friend, I'd accuse him of practicing.

WAITING FOR BEAUTIFUL

AUGUST

"Almost ready," I say to Grandpa, stretching a new piece of barbed wire across a metal fence post and clamping it in place. I look up at him and nod. It's blistering hot in the back pasture, and we've got more than a mile of fence to replace today. I have a sweat stripe down my back, and the sun reflecting off the new wire makes my eyes water.

"Hands free?" he says.

I hold my hands up so they won't get pinched when he pulls the wire tight. "Hands free."

Grandpa rolls the spool of barbed wire half a dozen paces to the next fence post.

We have been mending the pasture fences all week so they will be ready to hold the cattle when Frank, Jim, and John bring them down from the mountains a

121

few weeks from now. It's hard to believe we'll be able to keep cows alive on this land. After three straight months of hot wind, there isn't a living blade of grass, and even the crickets have moved away. I wipe the sweat off my face with my shirtsleeve. A few inches of good rain in September is all it will take, and the ground will be green and soft like summer never happened.

"Let's straighten up this post," Grandpa says. He pulls the leaning post upright. I jam pieces of shale from the ground into the hole at the base of the fence post, kick in some dirt, and stomp to pack it down.

"Better?"

"That'll do."

Grandpa cranks out a little more barbed wire, and I take the wire clippers from my belt. I clamp the wire in place, tighten it until it is level between the fence posts, and clip it.

"Hey!" Grandpa jumps back. The end of the barbed wire arcs through the air and snaps back with a metallic hiss.

"I'm sorry, Grandpa. I'm really sorry."

It's the second time I've made that mistake today. Grandpa has a rip down his sleeve and a cut on his arm from the last time I did it.

"Jeez, Dad would yell at me if I did the same stupid thing twice."

"Your dad made his share of mistakes."

"I bet he was better at this than me."

Grandpa straightens up and takes in the sky. "The question you want to ask yourself is not, Am I as good as my dad? That's just practice. Ask yourself, Do I love it as much as my dad? Talent is not your problem, Brother. Deciding what to do with your talents, that's the tricky part."

He takes off his hat and wipes the sweat off his head with a bandana. "Now tell me what you make of that sky."

He points to the thunderheads stacked on the eastern horizon, ash gray on top and olive green underneath.

"Wow, lightning for sure. Let's get all this metal off of open ground."

"Now you're talking like your dad. We can finish this job later."

We gather up our fencing gear and roll the spools of barbed wire across the pasture and into the barn.

Grandma is in the living room, sifting through the files, culling what we can't lose to fire and sealing it in a metal box. The radio drones out its usual country pop fluff, anchored every half hour with a weather and wildfire report. Grandpa heads out to mow the dead grass around the house down to a quarter inch of stubble. I fill the tub with clean water in case we lose power and the pump goes out. I roll up three sleeping bags and haul the emergency supplies out to the truck.

We've done this before. Every August, for as long as I can remember, the flames have touched down in another canyon, scorched someone else's land, devoured some other family's cattle and sheep. Custer, the barn cat, left first thing in the morning. Last I saw his ratty orange tail, he was scrambling up the rocks on the steep side of Red Rock Canyon.

That east wind picks up strong while we eat lunch, and carries the sound of thunder with it. I can see the horses in the corral cluster at the rail, eyes closed against the blowing dust and ears twitching in every direction. The cattle are going to be fine up in the mountains, but Ernesto and Donner have all the sheep at their summer grazing, maybe twenty miles northwest of the reservoir.

Ernesto took off weeks ago, with his bundle of gear strapped to the ATV and the new Stetson we got him for his birthday, smiling that broad, broken-toothed smile. You'd think he was the luckiest guy in the world, heading off for two months alone with Donner and 150 sheep, thirty miles from the nearest road. I try not to think too much about Bilbo and Frodo and short-legged Merry walking all those miles. Ernesto won't let them fall behind.

I load up the last of the emergency gear just as Grandpa is putting the mower back in the barn.

"The horses are dry," he calls to me from across the yard.

I head over to fill the trough just as a patrol car pulls into the driveway. Deputy Himmel leans a deeply freckled arm out the window, shouting. Grandma fills up a mason jar with water and joins Grandpa in the driveway.

"All the roads except 20 are closed," Deputy Himmel is saying. "There's emergency shelter at the fairgrounds in Burns. Winds are thirty miles per hour. You folks have fifteen minutes, tops."

"Lightning?" I ask.

"A dozen strikes at least, a few miles over." Deputy Himmel tilts his head to the east. He chugs Grandma's water with a grateful nod, spins in the gravel, and leaves. I search the east horizon. There's no smoke yet, and I don't smell anything but home.

The Grands trade a look. Grandma cradles his

wrinkled face in her hands, and Grandpa kisses her once.

"I'll get the horses," she says to him. "Did you raise Ernesto on the radio?"

Grandpa shakes his head.

"You'll find him," she says. "No one knows the land out there like you."

"Pigs and chickens," she calls over her shoulder to me as she heads to the truck and horse trailer.

There are just four old hens in the henhouse now, but I unlatch the door and shoo them out. Bacon and Sausage are pressing their fat shoulders against the gate and wrinkling their soggy noses at the wind. I have to set my boots and tug to get the gate open, but they head straight for the willow that hangs out over the creek. It's the coolest, wettest spot for miles around. The hens are already there.

"Guess you guys got the memo about the fire already," I say to them.

Grandpa is shouting and waving his hat at Spud, trying to load her up. Spud hates the trailer. All the other horses are bigger than her, and I think they tease her in there. Smoke is just starting to blow up the canyon. I dash in the house and grab four carrots from the fridge and a handful of bandanas from the laundry basket. I splash the bandanas with water and touch Dad's coat peg for luck on the way out the door. I tie a wet bandana over my face and drop one for Grandma on the open truck window. I hop in the trailer, whistle for Spud, and show her a carrot.

"Come on, Spud. Get in here." Spud snorts at Grandpa, but she hustles up the ramp to get my carrot.

"Get up, Patton; come on, Bradley," I call. Our cutting horses pile in.

"Get your saddle, Brother," Grandpa says. "There's no time for a second trip. We're going to have to ride Ike and Ginger out."

I open my mouth to protest, but he cuts me off. "Spud is too old, and you know it. She can't outrun a fire."

I know he's right, but Ike is Dad's horse. He's almost three hands taller than Spud, and he doesn't like me very much. I heft my saddle up on my shoulder, grab the blanket, and kick the barrel over to where Grandpa is saddling Ginger. The hot wind and smell of burning sagebrush have the horses twitching their heads around to find the danger. Grandpa's steady voice and firm hand keeps them in line. He holds Ike's head while I climb up on the barrel to throw the blanket and saddle over his back and cinch it down.

"Water," Grandpa says, and hands me both sets of reins. I lead Ike and Ginger to the trough and tie off the reins to the fence so they can drink. I run to the barn for canteens. Grandpa is already there, pulling out the Pulaski, a folding army shovel, the medical kit, and the surplus silver fire blankets. He rolls all of it into two tight bundles, and we head back to the yard.

I look over my shoulder at the house. The sight of it freezes me—Grandma's green checkered curtains at the kitchen window and Grandpa's black rocking chair on the porch. I remember the look on Dad's face the day he left for Iraq. He stood in the yard and studied the house one last time, memorizing exactly how everything should be. I feel that look all the way down to my toes. What if we never see it again?

Gritty black smoke swirls between me and the house, and I run for the horses.

Grandpa ties on the bundles. I stand on the barrel to climb up on Ike. Grandma has already pulled the horse trailer onto the road, a stack of heirloom quilts beside her and the cashbox on the floor.

"Meet you at the fairgrounds," Grandpa calls to her.

He turns Ginger, rides her across the pasture, and heads for the draw up Starvation Creek. Ike dances around like he's looking for Dad's weight, or maybe the sound of his voice.

I lean forward in the saddle and try to make my voice deep. "Aw, come on, Ike. Haven't I been taking good care of you? Get up now."

He turns his head around and gives me a one-eyeball stare.

"You aren't going to let Ginger get there first, are you? Look, she's getting away!"

That does the trick. He breaks into a canter and catches up to Ginger and Grandpa. We pick our way up the dry bed of Starvation Creek.

"Grandpa, what's Ernesto going to do? Does he know what to do in a fire? It doesn't exactly burn like this in Ecuador."

"He's as smart and careful a shepherd as I've seen, but if he's got the sheep up in the trees, we'll lose them for sure. On open ground, they have a chance."

We come out of the draw and onto the high table of land that sits between our ranch and the Strawberry Mountains. That hot wind pulls at my hat. Ike turns to protect his eyes. Smoke and dust sting my face. I can hear a sound to the east like a jet engine warming up. Grandpa sizes up our situation.

"When he checked in yesterday, Ernesto was ten miles northwest of here, headed toward Lookout Mountain." He turns to me. "Now remember, Brother, if the fire catches us, turn around and go back to the black. It won't burn twice."

I nod, cram my hat down tighter, and go. Ginger leads at a steady canter. Between the smoke and the thunderheads, it's like twilight an hour after noon, and the freight-train roar of flames gets steadily louder. I feel sweat rolling down my body and pooling at my belt and in my boots. Ike breathes hard. I squint against the smoke, sweeping the horizon for some sign of the sheep.

A dozen miles on, I see an ATV. I shout and wave Grandpa over. The ATV is parked on a granite outcropping, with a yard of bare rock all around it. It's ours. I recognize the gray-corded rosary Ernesto keeps wrapped around the gas cap. His supply roll is still strapped on the back. I knock on the water can and hear a high note.

"A couple of gallons left," I call to Grandpa.

"He wouldn't go far from his water," Grandpa calls back.

"Ernesto!" I holler. Coughing cuts off my yell, and I spit black snot. Grandpa takes a whistle from his pocket and blows, then stops to listen. A minute later, I hear Donner bark. He bounds out of the smoke from the northwest. His white coat is coal-miner black, but I'd know old Donner anywhere. He circles us once and takes off.

"We're coming, Donner!" I yell, and kick Ike to a full gallop. In a minute, I can hear the sheep.

A hundred yards further and I can hear Ernesto's deep, steady voice: *"Tranquilo, no temas."*

He has the sheep in a tight bunch, and he's trying to dig a fire line around them. For a second, I can only sit and stare. It's the most heroic thing I've ever seen. He could have left the sheep hours ago and been safe in Burns by now. But here he is, alone in the wilderness, fighting this war, just Donner and him, for sheep he doesn't even own.

"¡Hola!" Grandpa calls. He swings down from his horse with one smooth motion, unpacks the Pulaski, and tosses the army shovel to me. With a sweep of his arm, he shows that he gets Ernesto's plan and he's on board with it. He turns the Pulaski so the pick end faces down and the ax end faces up and begins to dig at the edge of Ernesto's line.

I run to the other side. Just as I'm about to dig, a wave of animals runs by: rabbits, mice, a porcupine, skunks, quail, a couple of coyotes, and a mule deer. Dread hits me. I look west, and for the first time I can see the red-orange line of flames. Donner circles the sheep, totally focused on keeping them together, and Ernesto's voice is still calling, *"No temas, tranquilo,"* just as solid and confident as a spring morning at home.

I start turning over dirt. The bitter taste of smoke is in my mouth, and I don't have enough spit to get it out. I can see Grandpa swinging the Pulaski. A wide sweat mark sticks his faded work shirt to his back. The knee-high flames pick up speed going up the little rise that's a hundred yards away. I can feel the heat on my arms and face. Bits of dead grass and tufts of wool start blowing toward the flames as they suck in air to fuel the fire.

We'll never finish the line. The fire is licking up the parched brown grass faster than sheep can run. Grandpa is kneeling on the ground, and I run to him to keep him up out of the flames. I am about to tug him by the arm when I see he's holding a match to a clump of weeds. It goes up like it's been drenched in gasoline.

"What are you doing?" I shout.

Grandpa ignores me. Ernesto takes one look at him, pulls out a lighter, and starts to do the same.

"Are you crazy?"

I run to the horses and lead them away, shooing the sheep back from the new fires that are only a stone's throw away. Grandpa and Ernesto stand up as the fires take hold. Grandpa leans a hand on Ernesto's shoulder. There is nothing but smoke and two lines of flame in front of us. There's no room to run. Fatigue washes over me, and every molecule in my body is screaming for water. Even Ike stands with his head down, like there's nothing to do but accept fate. I uncap the canteen and take slow swallows of warm water. I lift up Ike's chin and give him enough water to at least wet his mouth. He rubs my shoulder with his nose for thanks. I unpack Grandpa's canteen and a spare for Ernesto. The flames are just a few feet apart now. Grandpa takes the canteen and stares hard at the two lines of fire.

They meet up, and where they touch, the flames snuff out like a candle. Boom! and it's over—not even smoke, just a heat shimmer rising up from the black earth.

"Aha!" Ernesto dances in a circle, his palms up to the sky. He takes Grandpa by the shoulders and kisses each cheek. He spins me in a circle, laughing, but a tear slides down each side of his dusty face. He throws an arm over my shoulder like we are brothers, points to Grandpa, and says, "Wise old man. *Gracias. ¡Mil gracias!*"

I just shake my head. The fire sweeps on, a hundred yards away on either side, but we are standing in a golden patch of untouched prairie. The sheep are amazed to complete silence, and even Donner can see that none of them are going to wander off. He works his way to the middle of the flock, lies down, and falls asleep instantly.

I make a count of the sheep, keeping track on one hand of the ones that have my tag. Grandpa and Ernesto are deep in conference about where to take them. Water is only a few miles away, but they'll have to walk through the night to find grass that's not burned. Grandpa is massaging his left shoulder as he talks, like he's pulled a muscle. I gather up the tools, oven-hot from the ground, and look at the sky. It's hard to tell the storm clouds from the smoke, but the growl of thunder has moved up into the Strawberries, and the smoke has more of a brown-orange cast in the direction I'm guessing is west. I picture the BLM map Grandpa keeps on the wall in the hallway. Eighteen miles to Burns, maybe twenty, and I bet it's after three o'clock. It'll be dark before we get there.

Poor Grandpa; he looks dog-tired. Soot sticks in all the wrinkles that fan out from his eyes, making him look at least ninety. He lifts up the horses' hooves to check for splits and stones. Ernesto squats next to Donner, checking his feet for burns. I kneel and stroke the ashes out of his fur.

"Watch him," Ernesto says to me quietly. He lifts an eyebrow in the direction of Grandpa. "He need your strength to come home."

"Right." I shake my head. Grandpa splits logs every day with an ax I can't even lift. He can wrestle a two-hundred-pound heifer to the ground. I can barely tip over a sheep with a running start.

"No." Ernesto turns to me. He lifts up my chin. "Even the strong need help."

"Okay, okay," I say, but I see he's not satisfied, so I stand up and say, "I promise I'll watch over him like you watch over these sheep." I hold out my hand to shake on the promise. He takes my hand in both of his and shakes my arm up and down like a pump handle.

"*Sí,* now you're talking. *¡Fantástico!* You will be a shepherd to him."

Grandpa is already in the saddle when we walk up. Ernesto gives me a leg up and hands the canteen back to Grandpa. Ginger starts off at a trot, but we are only

a quarter mile on our way when he drops her back to a
walk. I pull Ike up next to him.

"That was really awesome with the fire, Grandpa.
How did you know it would work?"

He just grunts. His left arm hangs limp on the saddle bow.

"Are you okay? Did you hurt your arm?"

He gives a "yes" grunt. "Sore. Hurts."

"Do you want some aspirin for that, because I
probably have some in the—"

"Already took."

Pretty obvious he doesn't feel like chatting, so I
drop back and watch him. The smoke thins to almost
nothing as we move from scorched ground to dry sagebrush. The heavy clouds move north and the sun goes
below them on the western horizon, blasting me full in
the face. I tilt the brim of my hat and Grandpa drops
his head low.

"Sing," he says.

I know what he wants: the old hymns he sang
growing up in the Quaker church. We all used to sing
them together when I was little, before Mom left.
Grandpa led us in two- and three-part harmonies, his
own voice deep and true like a big church bell. He
doesn't usually ask me to sing. My voice doesn't go as

high as it used to or as deep as it should for the men's part. I start off with "Simple Gifts," and then I sing "For the Beauty of the Earth" and "Amazing Grace." I'm about to start another when Grandpa falls forward in the saddle and slumps onto the ground.

"Grandpa!" I shout. I jump off Ike and hit my knees in the dirt beside him. Ginger dances away, but then comes back and touches Grandpa's shoulder with her nose. She backs up and stands shoulder to shoulder with Ike, watching like people do when there is an accident on the highway.

As gently as I can, I roll Grandpa onto his back. He is groaning, with his right fist pressed over his heart. I search his body for blood or a sticking-out bone. Something I can fix. He grits his teeth together, groaning louder, and then gasps for breath.

"My heart," he pants. "Crushing me."

"No," I whisper. I unbutton his shirt at the top and wipe his face with my bandana. I search the horizon for somebody, anybody. There is no one to call. No help to run for. Only me to watch him.

"I'm here, Grandpa," I say, pulling off my shirt to pillow his head. "I'm right here." I remember what Grandpa said at Christmastime about angels being all around us when we need them, and I stand my ground.

I set my hand on his chest, and he grabs it. I can feel pain go through his body in waves. He squeezes my hand so hard, I can hear my knuckles pop. His eyes are shut tight, and tears roll down his cheeks.

I should pray. I start the rosary, stroking tears off his face like Dad did for me when I was little and afraid of the dark. I am just getting in the rhythm of shifting from Hail Mary to Glory Be when I remember that Grandpa likes the silent kind of prayer.

I stop and draw a deep breath. "Come, Holy Spirit. We are listening."

I take another deep breath, and Grandpa does too. I feel his muscles relax by inches.

"Listening, yes," he whispers.

"Are you all right now?" I whisper back. "Are you getting better?"

He shakes his head a fraction of an inch. "It's too heavy. Too heavy to take where I'm going."

He looks me in the eye and spreads my hand flat over his heart. I know exactly what he means, and even though I know I should fight it and tell him not to go and promise to save him, I just sit and hold his hand. His death comes to me like a true fact, like the last move in a chess game.

"I love you, Grandpa," I whisper. "I won't forget all the stuff you taught me to do."

"You are all good boys. Your dad, your brothers." He lifts up a last smile. "Sons to ease an old man's heart. And you, Brother, trying so hard to fill your dad's place. You don't have to be like him. You have your own road to follow. You'll know when you're ready." He coughs and closes his eyes. "You tell my bride, tell Miss Muriel Ann Casey—she is the most—"

And I wait for "beautiful," but it never comes. In that moment I feel heat and light push out of his body. It tingles up through my hand and makes my heart race. All the muscles on Grandpa's face go slack and, for a moment, I can see the young man he used to be. There is a glow around his body, and I feel hugged in by it.

And then it's gone, just like that, and I'm left with my hand over the shell of the body that used to be my grandpa.

I sit for what feels like hours. The sun dips lower and colors up the clouds gold and pink. My sweat dries to a salty crust, and the air gets cold enough to raise a shiver. I can't even believe what I'm feeling. Not angry; not even sad. Amazement, I guess. Honor at being a part of this moment. It's not like losing Pippin or any other animal. Not like it at all. I wait and watch the stars come out—Sirius to the southeast, and the Summer Triangle: Deneb, Altair, and Vega.

I let go of his hand.

By and by, Ike walks up. He comes slow, eyeing the body carefully. He sniffs and nudges it with his nose. He nips at the sleeve and then touches his tongue to the hand. At once he understands, and backs up a step.

It occurs to me why they always fade to black after someone dies in the movies. A dead person's body is a serious transportation problem. At least, it is out here. No ambulance; not even a car for miles.

"All right, God," I say, and I am a little mad because He was here an hour ago and now, just when levitation would be really helpful, He's nowhere in sight.

"Look, I can't leave him," I say. "There are scavengers out here, and bugs. How will I find him again? What will I say to Grandma if I don't bring him back? That's it. I'm staying until you find a way to get us both out of here, and if I starve to death, it's your fault."

That's when the miracle happens.

Ike steps up for one last sniff, and then he just lies

right down beside Grandpa's body. Unbelievable! I stroke his shoulder and look him in the eye to make sure this means what I think it means. Ike looks straight back at me and I remember. Grandpa was there with Dad the night Ike was born. He raised him from a foal.

I lift Grandpa's body by the shoulders and drape him over the saddle. It takes a lot of pushing and pulling, but I get him stomach-down across Ike's back.

"Good boy," I say, patting Ike's neck. "Up now."

Ike lurches to his feet, and I have to grab Grandpa's body by the knees and give him a good shove to get him balanced.

"Well, all right then, God. Thanks!" I say, too amazed to put more flower on that prayer. I take the reins and walk over to Ginger. She's much shorter and easier to mount, and Ike likes to follow her around. This might actually work.

It's pitch-dark, but I can still pick out west from the stars. A mile or so on and I can see the lights of the fairgrounds about eight miles to the southwest. There is no moon, but I search out the constellations Dad taught me and tell their stories for company. I am maybe a mile out of town when the Herdsman finally clears the horizon, and I think about why Dad and I chose this one, this shepherd of stars, to guide me.

And then, suddenly, I know, and it is exactly as Grandpa said. I've been on the right road the whole time. The secret of what I'm supposed to be is so last-chess-move perfect that I make up my mind not to tell anyone about it until Dad comes home.

COMING HOME

AUGUST

I'm not really one for making a flashy entrance. I like to slide in quietly and check things out first. But I bet people are out looking for Grandpa and me. Even though it's almost midnight, I don't think I have much chance of sneaking into the Burns fairgrounds quietly.

What am I going to tell Grandma? How can I explain what happened? I can hardly believe it myself, and I was there. Grandpa was fine galloping the horses out to find Ernesto and the sheep. He was fine digging a fire line to save them. It wasn't until all the danger was done that his heart gave out.

Hunger and thirst and fatigue make my head swim. The smell of horse sweat and smoke hangs in the air around me. I turn onto the county road that leads to the fairgrounds. I'm not on it fifty yards when a patrol car passes. It turns around and shines its headlights on me. An officer jumps out.

"Mr. Alderman? Brother? Is that you? Thank God!"

It's Deputy Himmel.

I still don't know what to say. Deputy Himmel runs up to the horses, lifts Grandpa's body by the shoulders to look at his face, and then lowers him gently back onto the saddle.

He turns to me and says, "Are you all right?" I nod, and he says, "Let's walk Mr. Alderman home."

He drops back and walks beside the horse that's carrying the body, with a hand on Grandpa's shoulder like an honor guard. Tired as I am, I sit up straighter because even though Grandpa has been hours in heaven, his body deserves the respect.

Deputy Himmel must have radioed ahead. When we get to the entrance gate, Grandma is waiting for us, along with all the other families in the valley that evacuated there to escape the wildfire.

It's me Grandma comes to first. I slide down from the saddle and Grandma is right there, hugging me tight and saying "Thank God" over and over again, and I say, "I'm sorry. I'm sorry, Grandma. I just . . . and then he . . . and I didn't know what to do."

"Don't be sorry," she says, stroking the ashes out of my hair. "He wasn't alone; I didn't want him to be alone. And you're here. You're alive."

She pulls back enough to look me in the face. "What would I tell your dad if I lost you?"

This I get.

"He found Ernesto and the sheep, and he saved them. He knew exactly what to do. And then, when it was all over . . ."

"His heart. I know."

"He said . . . he just thinks . . . you're really, really beautiful, Grandma."

And then she laughs and hugs me again, which is so like her, I feel a thousand pounds lighter.

The neighbors crowd in, kissing Grandma and shaking my hand. Grandma's best friend, Mary Gail, has her cell phone out seconds later and starts making arrangements to bring my brothers down from the mountains and get Pete home from Texas.

Paco and Rosita's whole family swarms us. If you are looking for loud lamenting, a Basque family is the way to go. Mr. Ugarte sobs openly, and all his brothers and sisters do the same. Rosita hugs me and gives me a kiss on the cheek, which isn't nearly as revolting as you might think, and Paco cries out loud, right in public—

brave as a lion. The girls from school slip in and take the horses off to the barns. I find an unlocked truck while everyone is still talking, curl up on the seat, and fall asleep in my boots.

Three days later, I'm sitting on the front porch, looking out over some other planet—a planet with no living plants and no Grandpa. Acres of river-bottom grass are nothing but a smudge of soot over bare dirt. The corral is outlined with the charred remains of the fence, and the horses stand inside purely out of habit. Frank is at the store with Mary Gail, getting what we need for the wake and funeral. Jim and John are fixing the pump. Grandma comes out to the porch with a damp dish towel and wipes the soot off the flag. She holds it out against the sky and gives it a critical look. It's only a little bit scorched on the bottom edge, and there are a few pinpricks of light that show through where sparks fell. It's like some extra stars have fallen in with the stripes. Grandma gives it a final shake and leaves it hanging in the still air.

I just sit and look at the charred ground and twisted metal that used to be the barn. There was a cottonwood shading the south side. It had a tire swing, and when I was little, Pete used to push me so high, my feet would reach the crown of the hills. The scorched skeleton of a trunk and one branch are all that remain. A lump of half-melted truck tire lies at the base. It's the tree that brought down the barn.

The house is heat-blistered but still standing, only because Grandpa spent his last hour at home mowing down the dead grass so it wouldn't carry the flames to the walls of the house.

Grandpa hated mowing. "That's what sheep are for," he would grump at Grandma when she made him trim the lawn for company. But he knew danger. I'm sure somewhere in his journals there is an accounting of every danger this family has faced and Grandpa's plan to fix it.

He knew it was a hazard to keep a tree near a building where a burning branch could fall and light up the roof. There's not even a shrub in reach of the house. But he knew I loved that tree and still rode the swing. I should have outgrown swing-riding years ago. Now there's nothing left of the barn except the concrete floor and a heap of scrap metal still warm to the touch.

Frank, Jim, and John came down from the mountains yesterday when they reopened the road to our place, and Pete just got in from Texas this morning.

Before, whenever the boys came home, there'd be a racket of teasing, bickering, and wild stories, and Dad and Grandpa would be right there, making us behave and putting us to work. Now it's tomb quiet, even with all five of us. We've become a house full of men who don't know what to say to each other.

After a while, Pete finds me. He's in his class B uniform for travel, with the light green shirt and the pants with a stripe and the shiny black shoes. I slide over so he can sit by me on the porch step. He's taller than Dad now, and their voices are so much alike I can't tell them apart on the phone.

"I'm going to miss that tree," Pete says, and tilts his head toward where the barn used to stand. "Grandpa used to push me on that swing sometimes when Mom was busy with the babies."

I just nod and lean my head on his shoulder because, honestly, I've never thought of what it was like for him to be twelve, like me, and have four little brothers tearing up the place. Loud, I guess.

Pete slides an arm around me and says, "Jeez, Brother, it was lightning. Even God doesn't know where lightning is going to strike. Nobody is mad at you, not about Grandpa or the barn or anything.

Besides, we can rebuild it. Dad and Grandma and I have a plan. "

"I promised," I say, and then I have to sniff up a whole glob of snot that suddenly appears in my nose. "I promised to take care of this place for him. I promised to keep it the same." I've been squeezing that thought in and swallowing it down ever since we got back to the ranch.

Pete must be able to tell, because he just nods and says, "You can throw up if you want. Might be a good time for it."

The minute he says it, I start gagging like a dog. Pete just sits there, patting me on the back like this is some kind of completely normal behavior.

A bunch of barfs later, Pete says, "Sometimes an empty stomach is better for news." He hands me his handkerchief to wipe out my mouth. "I just got off the phone with Dad. His plane landed in Germany an hour ago, and he'll be home late tomorrow. Father Ziegler is going to drive him here from Fort Lewis. He'll probably miss most of the wake, but he'll be at the funeral Saturday for sure."

Home—he's coming home! I never imagined it would be like this.

*   *   *

We spend hours getting ready for the wake. People and dishes of food arrive steadily. Jim and Frank set up tables in the yard. John and Pete get an extra generator running and string up outdoor lights. By late in the afternoon, cousins, nieces, and nephews roll in from Chicago and Boise and Yakima.

Everyone is quiet at first. They say their bit to Grandma and look at all the pictures of Grandpa, but pretty soon folks loosen up. Mary Gail steers them to the tables, and they get to work on the platters of sandwiches and covered casseroles that are stacked three deep on the kitchen counter. After supper, the stories start flowing. Folks get to laughing, and Grandma is in the thick of it, telling the wildest stories of them all.

Most of the evening, I just sit on the edge of things and take it in. I hear a dozen versions of the Grandpa stories I've known all my life: how he grew up on a dairy farm in Nebraska, how he met Grandma while he was driving an ambulance in World War II, how he faced down a cattle rustler in the fifties without even pulling out a gun, how he writes to Quaker pastors and senators and bishops, and even presidents.

I just float over the top of all this talk, putting in the nods and "ums" where they go. I can't believe Dad

is going to come home to this. I've imagined him coming home a thousand times—the parade, the spotless
house, the cows and horses healthy and strong, and all
the pieces of the operation in working order. Now he'll
come home to this—a burned-out ranch that looks no
better than a bombed street in Iraq. We've got a house,
but no barn. Horses, but nothing to feed them. The
pigs pulled through, but all that's left of the chickens
are a handful of feathers and coyote prints in the mud
by the river. The sheep will be fine with Ernesto, but
what on earth are we going to feed the cattle this winter, with all our hay burned up?

The wake goes on, and I'm glad it's getting dark so
Dad won't see the worst of it right away. Pete puts
some plywood over the burned grass in the front yard,
and pretty soon there is dancing and singing.

Dad comes home in the middle of it. I don't even
see him at first. I just hear a hundred separate conversations join into one cheer as Father Ziegler drives up
the gravel road to the house. Grandma gets to hug Dad
first. Apparently, this is something a hundred people
can agree on without talking about it, because everyone automatically stands back for her. But then Pete
pokes me out in front of him. When Grandma steps
aside, I finally get a full look at my dad.

He's not as tall as I remember. His face is browner than Ernesto's. He scoops me up in a hug like he used to and lifts me off the ground, but my toes dangle in the dirt, which they didn't used to. He has a lot more muscles than before, and his body smells like—I don't know what—not like anything around here.

He sets me down and says, so everyone can hear, "You brought your grandfather's body home and even wildfires didn't stop you. That was brave. Thank you."

If it was just him and me, I would have argued or at least explained that it was more a miracle, or at least a decision by his horse, Ike, than any doing of mine. I just tagged along and did the singing and praying. But he says it so stiff and formal in front of everyone that I don't know what to say. And then the moment passes, and the brothers crowd in for their hugs. I don't mind. I'm happy to stand back and watch while everyone else kisses him and asks their questions. Dad and I are going to have weeks, months—forever, really—after everyone else goes home.

Once the crowd thins out and the party moves to the cleaning-up-the-dishes part, Dad puts his arm over my shoulder and says, "Let's walk up to the reservoir."

I get a lump in my throat when he says it because

that's our star-watching place and I haven't gone up there in a whole year, not since before Dad left for Iraq. We walk away from the house, up the river, and then along the path that leads to a stretch of grass above the reservoir. He's walking a lot slower than he used to, and he brought a flashlight, which isn't like him either. The fire didn't make it up here so it's still green, which smells like heaven after the dry, ashy smells around the house.

I lie back in the grass, thinking about what I can say to him about that moment after the fire when Grandpa was lying on the ground and his soul left his body like rays of sunlight, and about the moment I knew for sure what I'm meant to become.

But Dad doesn't sit down with me, and before I can even begin, he says, "I've got three days. I'm sorry, son. I wanted to tell you before someone else does. It's just emergency leave. I have to go back the day after the funeral."

"What?"

I sit right up and stare at him. It can't possibly be true. We were barely making it with Grandpa's help.

"You're going to leave me and Grandma here alone? You already served longer than you are supposed to. It's not fair." I feel my muscles wind up tight like I'm getting ready to hit someone. "Why can't it be someone else's turn?"

Dad paces while I talk, and every little noise of a mouse or a bat makes him jump. Seems to me that even with all the extra muscle, he's not as solid as he used to be. I watch him peering into the dark shadows around the reservoir. I don't know what he thinks he's going to see.

"Be as angry as you want about me going back to Iraq, but I know you understand. I've heard the story about you and the wildfire from a dozen people tonight. Tell me this, son: Why didn't you and Grandpa get in the truck and go to the fairgrounds like everybody else?"

He says it almost like I'm a soldier of his and not his own boy.

"Jeez, Dad, Ernesto was out there all alone, just him and Donner and the sheep. We couldn't leave them!"

"So you rode out against an unstoppable force of nature. Why?"

"We didn't have to stop the whole fire, just the part of it that was close to our sheep. I didn't mean for Grandpa to die, Dad. It wasn't supposed to happen that way."

I look up and see that Dad is almost crying.

"My soldiers are still out there," he says, "and they are in danger every day."

I stand up and put my hand in his, because I do understand. It is breaking his heart to leave, but he'll never rest until they all come home.

My hand anchors him, and he stops pacing. After a minute, he sits on the grass and I sit beside him. We look up at the stars.

"One good thing about the desert, you can see stars from horizon to horizon; none of this mountains-cutting-off-half-the-sky business."

I move shoulder to shoulder with him and look up. The summer constellations are moving on and the fall constellations are rising, but I can still pick out the Summer Triangle.

"Deneb, Altair, Vega." Dad says their names solemnly, like a prayer. "I don't get much chance to go to church these days, but whenever I see those stars I pray for you."

I nod, thinking about all those three hundred–some nights that I searched for my Herdsman and prayed for Dad on the way in from barn chores at night.

He gives me a nudge with his shoulder and says, "Mostly, I pray my sons won't have to go to war."

"I thought you wanted us to go in the army. Why didn't you say something when Pete and Jim and John signed up?"

"I wasn't a veteran then. I don't want them to see the things I've seen."

"But, Dad, I finally decided what branch of the army I want to be in. It sort of came to me while I was bringing Grandpa's body home."

"You did? You want to be in the army?"

"Yeah. Chaplain Corps."

Dad smiles, and I can feel his shoulders relax a few inches. "Well, I guess I could make an exception for a priest in the family. Father Alderman—I like the sound of that."

"Are you surprised?"

"Maybe a little. I'm pretty sure your grandpa wouldn't have been surprised. He told me before I left that he wanted you to have this when he passed."

He reaches in his jacket and pulls out Grandpa's black leather journal. "There are about thirty of these altogether at the house, and they are all for you. Grandpa told me once that his father asked him to keep a journal when he got drafted back in 1943. Good advice. I've been writing in a journal, too. It has kept my feet on the ground and my mind steady during this command like nothing else has."

I flip on Dad's flashlight and open the book. There is Grandpa's typewriter-perfect print and a date on the top of the page. I always thought Grandpa was just writing about the events of the day in his journals, but the book is nothing like a diary. There are quotes from the Bible and what Grandpa thought about them; lists of books he liked; the names of people he prayed for; and the weather report, in a tidy two-inch square at the top of each page. It's like holding a handful of diamonds—my grandpa's whole prayer life in books that I can keep forever. I've only read a few dozen lines, but already I can hear his voice and feel his steady hand on my shoulder.

The first thing I think about when I wake up on the morning of Grandpa's funeral is the Mass, and making it his one last beautiful thing. Father Ziegler went over the Rite of Christian Burial with me yesterday, and we talked about some changes we will make to honor his faith and all his Quaker friends who will come.

I run through the parts of the Mass, lying on the top bunk because Frank insisted on the bottom one even though it isn't really his room anymore. Jim and John are doubled up in the other bedroom, and I don't think Pete slept at all. He was looking over Grandma's account books in the kitchen long after everyone was in bed, and he's up, talking on the phone now.

When I hear Grandma start her usual pot of morning oatmeal, I get up. John's in the kitchen, rattling pots and bragging on the cowboy griddle cakes he's going to make for all of us. Jim is eyeing the steak and eggs in the fridge. Me, I don't think I could get down toast and butter, but before we hit a full debate on the topic of breakfast, the ground starts shaking.

It's not the disaster-movie kind of earthquake, but a rumble strong enough to move my juice glass across the kitchen table in tiny hops. I jump up, jam my bare feet into boots, and run outside.

There is a long cloud of dust coming up the road, and out of it pulls a truck with four latrines on it. The potty truck pulls into our front yard. Right behind is a truck full of lumber, a flatbed with three months' worth of hay, a trailer with a dozen calves, and a school bus full of folks I've never seen before in my life.

Frank and Pete follow me outside, but Dad is already there.

"Who are these people?" Frank says.

The bus parks and the driver hops out. He is a serious-looking man not quite as old as Grandma, but definitely older than Dad. He walks right up to Grandma with his baseball hat in hand. There is another man about Pete's age right behind him.

"I'm Pastor Dale," the older man says, "from up around Cheney, Washington. It's a pleasure to finally meet you in person. When we heard about your troubles, ma'am, well, I just couldn't keep my congregation away."

"Pastor Warren, out of Lincoln, Nebraska, ma'am," the second man says. "Your husband was a mentor to me from my first year of seminary training. That man was a spiritual giant! Whenever I was in need of encouragement or wise counsel, a letter would come from this holy place and Mr. Alderman would be right there, helping me find my way."

He reaches out to shake Grandma's hand. She hugs him like he's one of the family and gives him a kiss on the cheek.

"Now, ma'am," Pastor Warren says, "I've brought a bunch of dairymen with me. We may never know the Scriptures like Mr. Alderman, but we do know a few things about raising a barn. I've got fifteen, and Pastor Dale brought twenty-three. We won't be able to finish a barn in two days, but we'll get up a frame and a roof. Now, that's a promise, ma'am."

Men start piling out of the bus, and women, too— sturdy folks with work gloves on and carpenter belts bristling with tools. It's like an army of angels, and right away Dad knows how to command them. He goes down the row, shaking hands. He gets Frank to fire up the coffeepots, and Pete starts filling the trough with water for the new calves. In a few minutes, everyone is standing in a big circle. Dad welcomes them and sets out the work schedule—what can be done in the seven hours before the funeral service, and then what we can finish up the next day. He's got a good voice for command—steady, clear, and organized. I see people around the circle thinking over his plan, nodding to buy in, and trusting it will turn out like he says. Dad was made to lead people. I can see it in the faces that look at him, and even more, I can feel it. It's just as much a part of him as this land and these animals. I'm never going to like it that he goes; maybe I don't have to. But command is a part of him, just like fire is a part of the land around here.

We are about to break up and get started when Pastor Dale calls out, "Who will lead us in prayer?"

I bow my head like everyone else. Only silence follows. I look up, and Dad is looking straight at me. A week ago, I would have been too nervous to pray out loud in front of strangers, but it is today, and I know the man I'm supposed to become. I close my eyes and lift up my hands to the hills around me in their black coat of ashes, still mighty, even though they've been through the worst thing that can happen to land. I bless this day, and the workers who have come from far away to build us up, and those soldiers who are still so far from home. I bless the man who carries the weight of commanding them and the memory of the man who prayed for peace. I bless this land, this ranch—always changing, and always home.

ACKNOWLEDGMENTS

I am grateful to the men of the 9th Engineer Battalion for bringing my husband home from the First Gulf War, and to my parents and the Herboth family, who walked me through Bill's deployment with grace and generosity.

I am grateful to the many writers from my hometown who have been supportive from the start, and to Oregon Literary Arts, which gave me the fellowship in 2005 that kept me writing. Thanks to Cheryl, Cliff, Lyra, Judy, and Kathie for their critiques and kind encouragement.

Thanks to Jim Thomas, my good shepherd of words. Most of all, I am thankful for my amazing family, who built me a tree house and made room in our lives for me to write.

Don't miss Rosanne Parry's next book,

SECOND FIDDLE

"If we had known that our discovery would eventually involve the Kremlin, the French ambassador to the United States, and the Joint Chiefs of Staff, we would have left that body in the river and called the *Polizei* like any normal German citizens. But we were Americans and addicted to solving other people's problems, so naturally we got involved. . . ."

Available from Random House in March 2011!